Snarling Death

He stood up slowly and turned his body just enough so that he could see. What he saw made him freeze.

It was a wolf, a great big, shaggy gray wolf. The animal's muzzle was wet and dripping with saliva, and its eyes were fixed on him.

He saw the wolf tense and knew he had to move now. Even as he drew, though, the wolf moved, rushing toward him and launching into a jump. He only had time for one shot, and almost as he fired the animal was on him. He felt the weight of the animal slam into him and was knocked off his feet, his gun spinning out of his hand . . .

Don't miss any of the lusty, hard-riding action in the Jove Western series, THE GUNSMITH

And coming next month:

THE GUNSMITH #73: APACHE GOLD

THE GUNSMITH

72
DAUGHTER OF GOLD

J. R. ROBERTS

JOVE BOOKS, NEW YORK

THE GUNSMITH #72: DAUGHTER OF GOLD

A Jove Book / published by arrangement with
the author

PRINTING HISTORY
Jove edition / December 1987

ISBN: 0-515-09329-7

Jove Books are published by The Berkley Publishing Group,
200 Madison Avenue, New York, New York, 10016.
The name ''JOVE'' and the ''J'' logo
are trademarks belonging to Jove Publications, Inc.

PRINTED IN THE UNITED STATES OF AMERICA

10 9 8 7 6 5 4 3 2 1

ONE

The Gunsmith had made love to many different kinds of women over the years, all colors, shapes, and sizes, but he couldn't recall ever making love to a woman as fat as Cissy DuPree.

Clint Adams was camped somewhere in the northern Dakotas, and the snow was falling. It was cold, and to combat the cold he made coffee, sat back, and thought about the last woman he'd had before starting his trek.

Cissy DuPree . . .

Cissy ran the whorehouse in Fort Clark, in the northern Dakotas. She ran three girls, whose task it was to handle all that the soldiers in the fort could hand her, not to mention the men from the small town outside the fort, and from the lumber camp.

They were real busy.

It was for that reason that Clint had to be satisfied scratching his itch with Cissy herself. The rest of the girls were too busy to go to bed with him for free, and he never paid for a woman. He never had, and he never would.

There were no other women in the fort, and pickings were slim in the town. For these reasons he had not had sex since arriving at the fort a month ago, and the itch was getting real bad.

He was in Fort Clark plying his trade as a gunsmith, but they said the real cold weather was coming and he wanted to get out before he got snowed in, so this was his last night in Fort Clark.

He wanted to be with a woman before he hit the trail, because who knew how long it would be before he got to a decent-sized town again.

He went to Cissy's that night and she greeted him with a mixture of delight and surprise.

"So," she said, "you've finally decided to come down off your high horse and pay for one of my girls, huh?"

"It's not a high horse, Cissy, it's just a rule of mine that I've kept for many years. Why pay for it when there's plenty of free samples walking around."

"You've been in Fort Clark long enough to know that free samples are at a premium, Clint Adams. The only choice stuff in town is in here. Now who will it be, Candy, Peaches, or Buttercup?"

Clint winced.

"I don't even like their names, Cissy."

"Makes them sound sweet, don't it?"

Clint had seen the three girls and they looked sweet enough without having to tote around names like that.

"I'm not here for one of them, Cissy."

"Then what? The only other gal in the house is me, and I quit taking johns a long time ago, Clint—not that I couldn't still show 'em a thing or two."

"Could you?"

"What?"

"Still show 'em a thing or two?"

She laughed, putting her head back. Cissy wasn't so much fat as she was big all around. Apparently, when she stopped taking johns she had also stopped watching her figure. It had been quite a nice figure in its time, but now it had filled out in all places. Still, even though she was big, she was firm-bodied. Big, creamy-looking breasts, wide hips, a waist that was in proportion to the rest of her, and solid legs. When you looked at her face you could see the pretty woman she once was, but now it was handsome, in spite of the fact that she had a little double chin, a wide jaw, and round, rosy cheeks.

"I know things I ain't even taught these girls yet, Clint—and I may never teach 'em. I don't think this poor excuse for a town is ready for that yet."

"Well, you wouldn't want to prove that to me, would you, Cissy?"

She stared at him in disbelief, and put her hand up against her breasts, right at the juncture where the two of them met. There was no valley there because her breasts were so big they swelled when they met. She looked to be about forty-five, but if she lost weight she might also lose ten years.

"Are you serious?"

"I am."

"You want to take me to bed?"

"Or the other way around."

"Why?"

"I've got a long trip ahead of me starting tomorrow. I want to spend a nice, warm, pleasurable night with a woman before I leave."

"And you don't want to pay, right?" Cissy DuPree said knowingly.

"I never pay, Cissy. If you're not interested, then I guess I'll have to do without. Or maybe you're not as good as you say."

"Even with all this weight I could show you more pleasure than one of these skinny—wait a minute." She closed one eye and looked at him suspiciously with the other. "You're trying to trick me into agreeing."

He shrugged and grinned sheepishly. "I guess I am. Sorry."

"You want me that bad, or do you just want a woman?"

"There are times in a man's life when all he wants is someone nice, uncomplicated, no strings attached—"

"You're on," Cissy said, putting her hands on her ample hips. Her upper arms were full and rounded, but there was no sag to them.

"You mean it?"

"Get your ass upstairs and see if I mean it."

"And no charge?"

"No charge. I'm gonna give you enough to last you a trip to Mexico from here."

"Jesus," he said, starting up the steps, "I don't want you to kill me."

"Too late, Adams," she said, walking behind him, "you've sealed your fate. You're going to have to prove to me that you can handle me."

TWO

Clint Adams had handled a lot of women before, but not a "lot of woman" like Cissy DuPree.

When they reached the top of the stairs she passed him and led him to her room. It was modestly furnished, except for the bed, which was a huge four-poster with a mattress that was thick enough to be a cloud.

"Just remember," she said, reaching behind her, "you asked for this."

She peeled her dress down to her ankles, revealing huge, pillowy breasts with dark brown nipples. The skin was smooth as silk, and white as milk.

He felt himself beginning to harden.

She was wearing a corset and she struggled with the strings on the thing, cursing, until she was able to get it off. She rubbed herself then, moving her hands over the marks the corset had left in her skin.

She was a solid woman with no sagging fat. In fact, undressed she didn't look all that fat at all, just big.

"You gonna stay dressed all night?"

He undressed, hanging his gunbelt on one of the two top posts. When he was naked she looked him up and down and whistled softly.

"Look at that. I got a stand out of you, didn't I?"

"You sure did."

"Yeah, it's standing right up there for little Cissy, ain't it, lover? Only Cissy ain't so little—and neither is this!"

She grabbed his swollen cock and rubbed her hands over it for a few moments, then went down to her knees heavily and took him in her mouth. She cupped his balls while she sucked him, licked him, and at one point began to hum while he was in her mouth. He felt an odd, vibrating sensation, and suddenly he was shooting into her mouth uncontrollably, and she was taking every drop.

"There," she said, "I'd say you were all done, friend, and not a challenge at all."

"You think so?" he asked, annoyed at being dismissed so easily.

"Then show me what you've got."

The bed was behind her so he put his hands on her breasts, cupping them, and pushed her down onto it, on her back. He joined her there and kissed her. She had full, firm lips, and her educated tongue poked right into his mouth without hesitation. It was the longest kiss he'd ever had, juicy and sweet and deep. When they broke the kiss they were both out of breath, and he could see Cissy's eyes glistening. He started to get hard again.

He went to work on her breasts, now. They were the largest breasts he'd ever seen or handled, but they weren't *fat* breasts, they were just big, firm ones.

He suckled the nipples until they were swollen, then ran his hand down over her swollen belly, into the forest of pubic hair, and poked around until his index finger encountered something hot and wet.

"All ready for me, huh?" he said.

"I'm ready for somebody, honey, and there's only you and me in the room."

He kissed her breasts and ran his tongue down over her belly into her pubic mound. Her flesh was soft, and she smelled clean. She had possibly the finest skin he'd ever seen on a woman. You could see the blue veins just beneath the surface.

"You have beautiful skin, Cissy," he told her.

"Forget the skin, baby," she said, putting her hands on his head and pushing down, "get to the red meat."

He ducked his head and did just that. His tongue encountered her moist lips and he licked them up and down, enjoying the taste of her. She spread her legs apart for him and he probed deeper with his tongue, causing her to jump. He ran his hands over her heavy thighs, up over her belly to her breasts, where he started to squeeze the nipples as he worked on her.

He teased her, licking her up and down, delving into her, all the time coming just so close to her clit, which by this time was rigid and straining for release.

"You bastard," she said breathlessly. "Oh you beautiful bastard. All right, so you're good, but do it . . . get to it before I— Ohhh, Jesus!"

He had cut her off and her exclamation was her reaction when his tongue finally hit her clit. He circled it with his tongue, sucked at it with his lips, then began to use his tongue to lash it. Finally, he closed his mouth over her and flicked his tongue back and forth, up and down, while she bucked beneath him, clutching his head, calling him names . . .

"Ahhh, Christ, I'm gonna . . . Jesus, here I go . . ."

She was a big woman and when the orgasm hit her she went wild beneath him. He tried holding her down, maintaining his contact with her clit, but he finally gave up. He thought the only way to stop her bucking was to get up on her and use his body weight. He climbed atop her, positioned himself, and then thrust himself into her, hard and fast, to the hilt.

She screamed.

She howled.

She bucked.

He pumped into her, then out, in and out, and she grabbed his buttocks and held them in her big hands, trying to pull him even deeper inside her . . .

Lying on top of her was like lying on a great, hot, overstuffed mattress.

It felt fine.

When he started to come she started to spasm all over again. She released his buttocks, grabbed his head, and kissed him hard, thrusting her tongue in and out of his mouth.

Later she got up on all fours and he took her from behind, with the aid of some lubricant she provided. He spread her huge ass cheeks, touched the swollen, slippery head of his cock to her anus, and then pushed.

She grabbed the top two posts and pushed against him every time he pushed into her. He held her hips tightly, then slid one hand around so that he could slide his fingers into her puss.

"Oh, Jesus, you rotten, stinking, lovely man!" she cried, and had another orgasm.

They were banging against each other so hard that the four-poster began to move across the floor.

"You . . . break . . . this . . . fucking . . . bed," she gasped, "and . . . and . . . I'll . . . Jeeeez!"

After that she lovingly cleaned his cock off for him, but when she was using a cloth to dry it, it began to stiffen again, swelling right in her hand. She quickly took it into her mouth again so she could feel it grow, then sucked him until he came . . .

"Well," he said later as they lay side by side in her big bed, "I guess you proved your point. I think I just got the best deal in the house."

Although it was as cold as a banker's heart outside, he was covered with sweat from his exertions.

"You weren't so bad yourself, Clint," Cissy said, just as sweaty as he was. "You know, if you came to work for me I'll bet we could draw a lot of women—"

"I appreciate the offer, Cissy, but I've got to get moving before the snow hits."

"I could think of worse places to be snowbound than here in this bed with you, Clint."

"You're a sweet woman, Cissy," he said, turning over so he could face her. He put his hand on her thigh and added, "I mean that in more ways than one."

"Have you ever had a woman as fat as me before, Clint?" she asked.

"You're not fat . . ."

"What would you call me?"

"Opulent."

"You sweet man! I think I love you. All right, as big as me, then."

"No, I never have," he said. "I never really looked at big women in that way, but now I see what I might have been missing."

"You ever fuck an ugly woman?"

Her casual use of whore-talk did not affect him adversely. If anything, it was quite the contrary.

"Not that I can think of."

"Come on, you've been with a helluva lot of women. I can tell. Not one of them was ugly?"

"Well, no. I mean, one of them had a front tooth missing, another was sort of short and stocky, still another one was almost fifty . . . but I can't say as I remember going to bed with an ugly one."

"Then you're missing a bet there, too. Any woman has a lot to offer any man, if she gets half the chance. You men, though, you only give the pretty ones the chance."

"Well, after this I think I'll be looking at women in a different way."

"Looking at them different is fine, lover," she said, rolling over to grab his semierect cock, "just don't *do* anything different than what you did here tonight. Promise me that?"

"I promise."

"Get some sleep now. I've got to go downstairs, and you have to get an early start. I'll wake you."

"My hotel—"

"Don't worry. They won't charge you for tonight. I'll see to that."

She got up and dressed and he watched her. He

never thought he'd enjoy watching a big, heavy, *healthy* woman get dressed, but he thoroughly enjoyed watching her. What a fine ass she had!

Cissy kissed him fleetingly and he was almost asleep before she got to the door.

"And don't forget," she called, "I'll wake you."

THREE

The next morning Clint awoke suddenly, feeling someone on the bed with him. Whoever it was was positioned between his legs, nudging his cock with a warm mouth to the first erection of the day.

He pulled the sheet away and saw Candy, one of the girls from downstairs. He then realized that Peaches and Buttercup were on either side of the bed, and now they got on with him.

They were all naked.

Clint had an acute sense of danger which would have awakened him immediately if it had been someone meaning to do him harm who had entered. Somehow, that extra sense of him knew that these women meant him no harm.

All three were naked, and as Candy took his cock into her mouth, the other two pressed against him with their breasts and thighs.

"What's going on?"

"Cissy said you were starting a long journey today. She said she wanted us to give you a send-off you would never forget," Candy said.

"And one other thing," Peaches said on his left.

"She wanted us to tell you," Buttercup said, her mouth against his ear, "that it's all free of charge!"

Clint threw some more wood chips onto the fire, which kept threatening to go out because of the wind and snow. He picked up the cup of coffee and wrapped his hands around it, seeking its warmth. Thoughts of Cissy and her three girls were pleasurable, but they did nothing to keep him warm.

He turned to look at the horses—his team, and Duke, his big black gelding—and envied them. Horses handled the cold a lot better than humans did.

Clint didn't handle the cold at all, but he had been in Wyoming when he got word from Fort Clark from a friend of his, Lieutenant Sam Butler, that his expertise with guns was sorely needed there. An army gunsmith had been sent to the fort, but he'd been robbed and killed on the way, it would be some time before another could reach Fort Clark.

Clint responded to his friend's call, as he always did for his friends, and that's how he had gotten himself in this predicament. He was camped right smack dab in the middle of a snowstorm that was so heavy it almost blinded him.

"Damn," he said, dumping the remains of his coffee into the fire. "It might just as well be night. Come on, Duke, let's get moving anyway." Night or snow, it don't make any difference, traveling would be just as treacherous, but he couldn't just sit here and freeze to death.

He hitched up the team and started forward, hoping against hope that the snow would let up long enough for him to get to a more decent climate.

FOUR

Papa Teng thought the man was dead.

The horse, however, a huge black beast, was definitely alive, and standing over the man as if he were protecting him from potential harm.

Papa Teng hurried over to him, followed by his sons, Chang and Ling, fourteen and sixteen years old respectively. He was about to touch the man when the horse made a sound that Papa Teng took to be a warning.

"I am not going to hurt your master," Papa Teng said to the horse. "I want to help him. Do you understand, beast? I want to help."

Papa Teng didn't know if the great beast understood or not, but this time when he reached for the man the horse made no sound.

Papa Teng turned the man over and put his head against his chest.

"Is he dead, Papa, is he dead?" Chang asked anxiously.

"Hush."

Papa Teng listened for a very long time, and was rewarded with a heartbeat. The man was frozen, and who knew how long he had lain out here, but he was still alive. Now Papa Teng knew that they had to get him to the house, where he could be properly tended to by his wife, Soong.

"Come, help me put the man on his horse."

Chang was little help in lifting, because he was so small, but he helped by holding the reins of the big horse. That is, he *thought* he was helping, but Papa somehow knew that the horse would not move until his master was securely on his back.

For sixteen, Ling was a large boy, and strong, and between them he and Papa Teng got the man on the horse's back crosswise. Using the man's own rope Papa lashed him to the saddle, and then addressed the horse.

"Come, great beast, and we will take your master to safety. Come."

Papa tested the reins—and the horse—by pulling ever so slightly, and was rewarded when the horse took a step forward.

"Good," he said, "good. Come, we go now."

He pulled and the horse followed, so he and his two sons walked the man and his horse to the house the Teng family was using.

"Run and tell Mama so she will be prepared," Papa told Chang.

"Yes, Papa."

Chang was only too happy to be the one to tell his mother about the *lo fan*, the white man they found during their hunting, lying on the ground, frozen, almost dead.

When Papa and Ling reached the house they were greeted by Soong Teng and her eighteen-year-old daughter, Donna. (Her real name was Sooni Teng, but lately she had insisted that her family call her by her chosen American name. She said that since they had chosen to live in America, they could all have American names.)

"Bring him in, put him on the bed."

"Put him on my bed," Donna Teng said. "It is the closest."

Papa Teng and Ling got the man off the horse, and then the whole family aided in carrying him inside and putting him on Donna's bed, in her room.

"Ling, go and tend to his horse."

"The great beast will bite me."

"Ha, he is afraid! I am not!" shouted his younger brother.

"The great beast will not bite you. Now go and do as I say!"

"Yes, Papa."

"I will help."

"I don't need any—" Chang began to answer, but soon the two boys were out of earshot.

Thankfully.

"Move away from him, Papa. I will take care of him. The poor man is almost frozen."

Papa Teng moved away and watched with admiration as his wife, Soong, took command of the situation. Was it any wonder he loved her?

"Yuen—uh, Donna, go and get some blankets. Papa, boil some hot water. We must warm him."

"Will he live, Mama?" Donna Teng asked, looking

down at the unconscious man.

"I believe so. He is young, and probably strong."

"He is so handsome," Donna said.

"Get the blankets as your mother told you," Papa Teng shouted from the stove.

He wondered now, for the first time, if he had made a mistake in bringing the man here. Who was he? And what if he worked with *them*?

These were questions that would not be answered until the man woke up.

If he ever did.

FIVE

It took a couple of days, but Clint Adams finally did wake up.

When he did he saw a lovely Chinese girl looking down at him with a concerned look on her face.

"You are awake?" she asked.

"My eyes are open, aren't they?"

She gave him a stern look now and said, "Your eyes were open two other times, as well, and you weren't awake."

"Did I speak either of those two times?"

"No."

"Well, then, I must be awake."

"I will call my father."

"Wait," he said, grabbing her wrist. "What happened? Where am I? Who are you?"

"All your questions will be answered after I have called my father." She looked down at his hand as it held her wrist and said, "Please?"

21

He released her, and mumbled, "I'm sorry."

He watched her as she left the room and then began to check himself for damage. He moved his feet, then his legs. So far so good. He flexed his fingers, moved his arms, then used his hands to feel himself and make sure everything was where it should be.

After that he started trying to remember what had happened.

He remembered a lot of snow, and the team had started to complain. At one point they had stopped cold, refusing to move. He had climbed down from the wagon and gotten in front of them to try and coax them into moving. When that didn't work he started to climb back aboard the rig, and the team had chosen that precise moment to move. The rig had jerked, and he had fallen, and . . . and then what?

He put his hands to his head and eventually found the soft area behind his right ear. So, he had fallen and struck his head. Obviously, he had been knocked out, but for how long? And who had found him? The girl's father? And he had brought him here?

He started to get a headache, and he became aware of a numbness in his legs. At that moment the girl returned with a gray-haired Chinese man behind her.

"Are you still awake?"

"I think so."

"This is my father."

"Does he have a name?"

"Papa Teng," the old man said. "You may call me Papa Teng."

"My name is Clint Adams. Are you the one who found me?"

"Yes," the man said softly. "My son Ling and I found you lying in the snow. Your horse—"

"Duke—that's my horse. Is he all right?" Clint asked with concern.

"Your horse is fine. He stood guard over you well, but allowed me to approach."

"He knew you meant me no harm."

"He is a remarkable animal to have such instincts."

"Yes, he is. I figure I fell from my wagon and struck my head."

"Yes, that is how I reconstruct the events. There was a large rock near where you were lying."

"What about my team, and my rig?"

"We found your wagon lying on its side about two hundred yards from where we found you. But we never found your team. The wagon evidently became stuck and as they pulled it fell over, freeing them."

"How bad is the wagon damaged?"

"I cannot say. We have not been able to raise it to a standing position."

"If you'll help me maybe we can—" Clint started, making to rise, but the old Chinaman put his hands on his shoulders and, with surprising strength, prevented him from doing so.

"You must lie still. You have not yet fully recovered from the frostbite."

"Frostbite?"

"Apparently you were lying there quite some time when we found you. Your feet and legs were very cold, possibly frostbitten. I am not a physician, but I did what I could. How do your legs feel?"

"A little numb, but I can feel them. I guess you did pretty well, huh?"

"I did my best."

"It was good enough." Clint looked at the girl, who appeared to him to be seventeen or eighteen. She was also extremely pretty. "And what's your name?"

She opened her mouth to answer, but her father answered for her.

"She is Sooni Teng, my daughter."

"I prefer to be called Donna," she added, smiling.

"All right, Donna. I guess if your father was my doctor, you were my nurse, right?"

"She and my wife, Soong Teng, stayed by your side while you have been here."

"How long have I been here?"

"Two days."

"And where is here?"

Papa Teng shrugged his shoulders.

"A cabin in the mountains."

"Are we still in the Dakotas?"

Papa Teng nodded.

"Nebraska is about fifty miles south."

Clint nodded. He would have liked nothing better than to spend this winter in New Mexico, and as soon as he was able to travel, that's where he was headed.

SIX

That evening Clint decided that he was going to get up and walk to the dinner table to eat with Papa Teng and his whole family. Papa Teng advised against it, but Clint insisted on it, and Papa just stood back and watched as Clint stood up, then fell down.

"Jesus!" Clint said from the floor. His legs felt like wet noodles.

"Sooni will bring your dinner after we have finished eating," Papa Teng said, and left without helping Clint up.

"Tough little Chinaman," Clint muttered, crawling back into bed.

About half an hour later, Donna Teng came in carrying a bowl of soup.

"I have your dinner."

"Thank you."

She sat on the bed, and as he reached for the bowl, she said, "I will feed it to you."

Remembering what had happened when he tried to stand up, he decided not to try holding the bowl of hot soup.

"Do you have any brothers and sisters?" Clint asked between spoons of soup.

"I have two younger brothers, Ling, who is sixteen, and Chang, who is fourteen."

"Are they the ones who hauled me in?"

"Yes."

"I'll have to meet them and thank them."

"You will meet them. They are very curious about you."

He accepted a spoonful of soup and then realized that there was something that he hadn't asked yet. He must have *really* hit his head hard and addled his brain to have neglected to ask the question before now.

"Donna?"

"Yes?"

"Where's my gun?"

"It is under the bed."

"Would you take it out for me, please?"

"Finish your soup—"

"First the gun . . . all right?"

She glared at him and then said, "Oh, all right."

She put the soup down on a nearby table, then got to her knees to retrieve the gun and holster.

"It was not damaged," she said, handing it to him.

Clint took the gun, unwrapped the gunbelt from around it, and examined it well. He decided that he would have to clean it very soon, just to make sure it was in proper working order.

"Now will you finish your soup?"

"Sure," he said, putting the gun down beside him on the mattress. "It's very good."

"My mother is a very good cook."

Clint finished the soup, then asked Donna if her mother made coffee.

"Papa does not drink it, but I could bring you a cup of tea."

"Tea?" he asked. "All right, I guess you can bring me a cup of tea."

Donna left and Clint checked the action on his gun. It was a little sluggish. He was going to have to ask Papa Teng to bring his gunsmithing tools in from his rig, if he hadn't already done so.

Donna entered carrying a cup of tea and said, "My brothers would like to come in and meet you."

"Sure, send them in."

"First Papa would like to talk to you."

"All right."

He accepted the cup of tea just as Papa Teng entered the room. He said something to Donna Teng in Chinese and she left the room.

"She's a wonderful girl."

"Yes, she is," Papa Teng said. He had a stern look on his face, and Clint suspected that he was going to bring up a fairly serious subject.

"My sons would like to meet you, Mr. Adams."

"Donna told me that. Trot them on in, Papa Teng."

"In a moment I will . . . bring them in, but first I wanted to talk to you."

"Donna said that, too. What about?"

"You are obviously a man of violence, Mr. Adams—"

"What makes you say that?"

"Your wagon is filled with guns, and you wore a gun when we found you. Also, you now have your gun on the bed with you. I do not have any guns in my house."

"Well, I think you're judging me rather harshly," Clint said, although considering his reputation, he couldn't argue all that hard. Still, it didn't sit right with him to be condemned for the wrong reasons.

"My wagon is filled with guns, Papa Teng, because my business is fixing guns."

"That may be so, but a man who must have a gun in bed with him is a man of violence. Do you not have a reputation as such?"

Clint wondered if Papa Teng had recognized his name at some point, or if he was just making deductions based on what he saw.

"Yes, Papa Teng, as a matter of fact I do have a reputation, but—"

"It is as I suspected."

Clint opened his mouth to argue, then decided that it would be futile. He might as well let Papa Teng get whatever he had to say off his chest.

"My sons are sixteen and fourteen years old, and are very impressionable. I would prefer it if you did not regale them with stories of your violent past."

"Whatever you say, Papa Teng. This is your house, and I am just a guest—and possibly an unwanted one."

Papa Teng did not reply to that.

"I will bring my sons in to meet you."

"Fine."

Papa Teng went out, and Clint put his gun next to him, but underneath the blanket. He wondered why Papa Teng had warned him about his sons, but not about his daughter.

Papa came in with the boys, one of whom was taller than he was. Clint assumed that this was sixteen-year-old Ling, and the other was fourteen-year-old Chang.

Papa Teng introduced the boys and stood by while

Clint asked them questions, never giving them an opportunity to ask him questions. This seemed to meet with Papa Teng's approval.

"I want to thank you boys for saving me from a cold grave."

"We were happy that we could help," Ling said.

Chang simply nodded. Apparently these boys had not seen a stranger in quite a while. Clint wondered what Papa and his family were doing in these mountains.

"That is all for tonight, boys," Papa Teng said. "We must allow Mr. Adams to get his rest."

The boys obviously wanted to stay longer, but they dared not argue with their father.

When they were gone, Clint said, "They appear to be good boys."

"They are."

"And you want them to stay that way."

"Yes."

"As soon as I can ride I'll be moving on, Mr. Teng. You don't have to worry."

"You will not leave until you are well enough," Papa Teng said. "I have never forced anyone to leave my house before they were well enough."

"I appreciate that. I appreciate everything you and your family have done for me, Papa Teng."

"Then all I ask in return is that you not fill their heads with stories."

"I have no stories to tell, Papa Teng," Clint said. "Not to children."

Papa Teng nodded and started for the door.

"Would you be able to get me something from my wagon?"

Papa Teng said, "What do you need?"

"My tools, gunsmithing tools. I'd like to work on my gun."

Papa Teng's jaw hardened but he nodded and said, "I will bring them to you in the morning."

"Thank you."

After Papa left, Clint lowered the flame on the storm lamp on the table next to the bed, took his gun out from beneath the blanket, and closed his eyes.

SEVEN

The next morning Donna brought Clint breakfast and Papa Teng brought him his tools. Clint ate the breakfast, but was happier to receive the tools. He cleaned his gun thoroughly, returning it to perfect working order.

He had been able to feed himself, so Donna had left him the food. When she came to collect the dishes he asked her a question.

"Where's my horse?"

"There is a small shed in the back of the house. He is in there, away from the snow."

"Is it still snowing?"

"It stopped yesterday."

"Are there any other houses around?" he asked. "Somewhere we could get help in standing my wagon up?"

"No," she said, "no other houses. There is no one else around."

"Must get kind of lonely, especially for a pretty girl."

She touched her face, reacting as if no one had ever told her that she was pretty.

"What are you and your family doing up here, Donna?"

For a moment she seemed poised to say one thing, but then changed her mind and said, "I cannot say. Papa would be very angry."

"That's all right, Donna. Thanks."

At the very least, she had told him that there was something to be learned, something that Papa Teng did not necessarily want him to find out. Obviously, the longer he was there, the more chance there was of him learning what it was—if he wanted to.

Donna left and Clint experimented with his legs. He swung around so that they touched the floor and then put pressure on them. They seemed to hold up fairly well. Next he tried standing, and although he was a little shaky, he remained on his feet. He took a few steps, then got bolder and walked to the window. Outside the ground was covered with snow, but the weather was clear. There was even some sunlight.

Donna came in just then and Clint turned to face her. He was wearing only his long johns, but knew it would be futile to try and cover up.

"My mother wants you to know that she will make you coffee if you wish it."

"Tell your mother thank you, I'd like that very much," he answered.

"I will tell her."

"When will I get to meet your mother?"

Donna shrugged.

"Maybe the first time you are able to eat at the table with us."

"That will probably be tonight, then."

"I will get the coffee."

She turned and left, and Clint wondered why a girl of eighteen who had apparently led a sheltered life had not been embarrassed to find a man standing in his long underwear.

EIGHT

Donna came in about ten minutes later carrying a large mug of coffee. By then Clint was back in bed with his gun by his side. It seemed ludicrous to keep it handy under these conditions—being alone in a house with an old Chinese man and his family—but the most innocent of conditions had often turned dangerous within the wink of an eye.

He saw Donna look at the gun when she handed him the coffee, but she didn't ask about it.

The coffee was black and strong, and he commented on it.

"It's the way I like it."

"That's what Mama said," Donna said, sounding puzzled, "that you would like it strong."

"Your mother is a pretty smart lady. Is she as pretty as you?"

Again, when he mentioned her beauty, she touched her face.

"My mother is beautiful."

"Then you take after her."

"I—I have work to do. I will come back for the cup later."

"All right."

She left and he drank the coffee. He was setting the mug on the table next to the storm lamp when he saw some movement by the door. He watched and saw it again, a head coming into view, and a pair of eyes peeking in.

Chang, the fourteen-year-old.

"Come on in, Chang."

The boy pulled his head in, then shyly stepped into the doorway, his hands behind his back.

"Come in."

"Papa says we are not to bother you."

This one looked like his sister, which meant he favored his mother. Ling, the older boy, looked like a larger version of his father.

"You're not bothering me. I could use someone to talk to."

The boy took a few tentative steps forward, but once he was in the room must have figured that if he was in for a penny, he was in for a pound. His steps were more sure as he walked to the bed.

"My name is Clint."

"Mr. Adams."

"You can call me Clint."

"That would not be showing you the proper respect."

"Did your father tell you that?"

"Yes."

"Well then, he's right."

Clint realized then that he had made a mistake. He

saw the boy looking at the gun on the bed next to
him. He could have tucked it away beneath the blanket, but yanking it from the boy's view suddenly would
only increase his curiosity.

"What are you supposed to be doing right now?"
Clint asked Chang.

"My chores."

"And why aren't you?"

"I was curious . . . about you."

"Why?"

"You are a stranger. I have not seen many strangers
since we came here."

"When was that?"

"A month ago."

"Then this isn't your home?"

"No."

"Where is home, then?"

"We do not have a home, Mr. Adams. We lived for
a while in San Francisco, where my mother and father
had a laundry, and then my father worked the railroad
and we moved around."

"Why did you come here, then?"

"I do not know. We came here because my father
said we must."

"And no one questions your father?"

"No one," Chang said solemnly.

"Not even your mother?"

"My mother is just a woman."

"I see."

The boy was starting to get nervous now, shifting
from one foot to the other.

"You'd better go and get those chores done before
you get caught, Chang."

"You are right, Mr. Adams."

He turned and ran for the door, then stopped and turned to smile at Clint and said, "See you later . . . Clint!"

Clint laughed and lay back in bed. He took his hand away from his gun and laced his fingers behind his head.

Why would a man take his family and isolate them in a house in the mountains? There were still railroads to be built, and Clint was sure that a Chinaman couldn't make better money working anywhere else. So why abandon that work and come up here?

The answer was fairly simple. There was something up here, nearby, that was worth more to Papa Teng than what he could make working for the railroad.

Like what?

Clint wondered if there had been any gold strikes in these mountains that he hadn't heard of.

Or was it something else?

Curiosity was getting the better of him, and that was bad. It was none of his business, but just lying there in bed there was nothing else he could do but wonder about it.

He got up again and walked back and forth, trying to work the strength back into his legs. He had to get up and about, get his wagon righted and see what damage had been done. There was probably more snow coming, and he didn't want to get snowed in here. Not with Papa Teng and his family and his mystery.

His family was fine, but his mystery was his own, and Clint wanted no part of it.

Even if he was curious.

NINE

That evening Donna came and asked him how he felt.

"I feel better."

"Would you like me to bring you your dinner?"

"I think I'd like to come out to the table to eat it, if it's all right."

"I will tell Mama to set another place."

When dinner was ready it was Ling, the older boy, who came in to get him.

"You can lean on me, Mr. Adams."

"I can walk, Ling."

"I am strong," Ling insisted. "You can lean on me."

"I know you're strong, son, but I have to get strong, too, and I can't do that by leaning on you." The boy looked disappointed at not being able to show his strength, so Clint added, "But stay by me, because if I start to fall you can catch me."

"I will catch you, don't worry."

Clint walked all the way to the table and sat at a place that had been set for him. When Papa Teng's wife came to the table with the food, he got his first good look at her.

Donna had been right. Her mother *was* a beauty, and she appeared to be almost twenty years younger than her husband. She had long dark hair that was parted in the center, a round face with high cheekbones, lovely eyes, and a full, generous mouth. In a few years Donna would look just like her, and at some point might even surpass her in beauty. The young girl had the same dark hair and full mouth, but there was still some baby fat on her, enough to almost hide the cheekbones he knew had to be there.

They were the same height, but the mother was fuller in body than the daughter. The mother must have been very young when Sooni was born, because she looked barely forty now.

"This is my wife, Soong Teng."

"It's my pleasure to meet you, ma'am. I thank you for all you've done."

She merely bowed to him and set the food on the table. She sat and waited for her husband to serve their guest and then himself before taking her own food and starting to eat. Apparently, she was totally subservient to her husband.

There was no conversation at the table, but there was tension in the air. Clint thought that he might be the reason for both.

After dinner, mother and daughter began to clear the table, and at one point Soong Teng spoke, as if she could hold herself back no longer. She also looked frightened.

The conversation was short and angry, and totally

in Chinese. From what Clint could gather Soong Teng wanted her husband to do something, and he simply refused to do it, or discuss it.

"I apologize for my wife's lack of manners," Papa Teng said.

"Her manners seem fine enough to me."

"She should not have spoken so."

"I didn't understand, anyway."

"She still should not have spoken."

"What was it about?"

"It does not concern you," Papa Teng said, and his tone was without offense. It was a simple statement of fact, and one that Clint could not argue.

"You're right, Papa Teng." He stood up and said, "I think I'll go back to bed. Tomorrow I may be ready to ride."

Papa Teng shook his head.

"Tomorrow you may be ready to walk outside, and possibly even walk to where your wagon is, but you will not be able to travel yet."

"Maybe," Clint said. He started back to his room— he wondered who usually slept there—and Ling quickly rushed to his side.

"I will catch you, Mr. Adams," he said, "if you fall."

"Thanks, Ling."

Back in bed Clint thought it over. Obviously Mrs. Teng was afraid of something and possibly wanted Papa Teng to talk to Clint about it, maybe ask for his help.

No, he was going to stay out of it, whatever the problem was—unless Papa Teng asked for his help. He couldn't refuse then, because he owed the man his life.

Still, if he could leave before Mrs. Teng could convince her husband to talk to him he'd be able to stay out of it.

Who was he kidding? He hadn't been able to stay out of trouble—his own or somebody else's—for years. That was part of having a reputation.

He lay back and closed his eyes. Maybe, come morning, he'd be strong enough to leave.

Maybe . . .

TEN

Later, after dark, he sensed that someone was in the room. His gun was on the bed next to him. He touched it, but did not close his hand around it. With his other hand he reached for the storm lamp and turned the flame up, lighting the room.

It was Soong Teng, Papa Teng's wife.

"Mrs. Teng—"

"I must talk with you," she said in a low voice.

She was dressed in her nightclothes, and her long hair had been tied into a braid. Her hair was parted down the center. She had her hands in the pockets of her robe, and her shoulders were hunched, as if she were expecting a blow.

"Talk, then."

"We have much trouble."

"Sit down and tell me about it."

"If my husband knew I was here he would be very angry."

"Where is he?"

"Asleep. He is a very sound sleeper. He works very hard all day and sleeps very well at night."

There was a chair in the room, but instead of sitting there she sat on the bed. He felt the warmth of her body against his leg and moved to break the contact.

"I do not know where to start."

"Why are you here?"

"When my husband worked on the railroad a man told him about some gold that he had stolen. He told my husband where he hid it."

"In these mountains?"

She nodded.

"But not the exact location?"

"No."

"Who was the other man?"

"Just a man, a countryman named Khan, who became involved with the wrong people. There was a robbery, the other men were killed, and Khan escaped with the gold. He was frightened then, so he hid the gold and left it there, afraid to touch it for fear that he would be caught and killed."

"Why did he tell your husband about it?"

"They became very good friends, and were going to go and get the gold together."

"Khan was going to share the gold?"

"Yes, he said he would."

Clint had never heard of anyone willingly sharing something he already had—especially gold.

"What happened then?"

"Someone killed Khan."

"Someone with the railroad crew?"

"Yes, it had to be. He was found one night badly beaten."

"Why was he killed?"

"No one knew, but my husband suspected that someone else knew about the gold and was trying to get Khan to tell where it was."

"Did your husband suspect anyone?"

"Yes, a terrible man named Landergott. He also worked on the railroad crew."

"Now you're afraid that Landergott is coming—or is he already here?"

"I am fearful that he will come and kill my husband."

"He won't do that, Mrs. Teng, not until he finds the gold. Your husband is the only man who has any idea where it is, right?"

"Yes. He was given some landmarks to look for."

"And that's what he's been doing here for the past month? Looking for the gold?"

"Yes, with my sons. There are many caves in this mountain, and they must look through all of them."

"Will you tell your husband that you told me all about it?"

"Tomorrow," she said, nodding her head. "He will be angry, but I must tell him."

"Why did you tell me?"

"My husband says that you are a man of violence, a man who knows how to use a gun. We need such a man to protect us against Landergott."

"What makes you think I won't steal the gold?"

"I see the way my children react to you. You are not a man who would kill children, or steal from them."

"And Landergott is?"

"He is a dangerous man, a violent man—violent with his hands, and with a knife."

"And a gun?"

"Yes."

"What else?"

"He . . . said things to me, put his hands on me. My husband is . . . older than I am, Mr. Adams. Landergott would kill him easily, and yet if I told my husband the things Landergott said, he would fight him."

"Are you telling me that Landergott wants you as well as the gold?"

"Me, or Sooni. He made that clear enough times. He said if he couldn't have the mother, he would take the daughter."

"Will Landergott be alone?"

"He has friends who followed him."

"How many?"

"Three, four."

"So there's a possibility that we're talking about five men with knives and guns."

"Yes."

"Were they still with the railroad when you left?"

"Yes, but they will follow us. I am sure they will follow."

"What does Landergott look like?"

"He is about thirty-five, tall, ugly, with blond hair and a scar over his right eye that causes the eye to stay slightly closed. An ugly man!"

Clint thought she was right about Landergott following them. When men like Landergott smelled blood — or gold — they usually stayed on the trail for as long as it took.

If they weren't already here. After all, they'd had a month to catch up to the Tengs. Clint didn't say that to Mrs. Teng, though.

"Mrs. Teng, in order for me to help, your husband

will have to ask me. He strikes me as a proud man."

"He is, proud and stubborn, but if you insisted on repaying us for . . . saving your life, then he might consider asking you . . . don't you think?"

"What little I understand about Chinese culture, he would have to be sure that I was an honorable man, and honorbound to repay the debt."

"Yes, you are correct. Once he is convinced that you are an honorable man, he will not be afraid that you will steal the gold."

Clint nodded his understanding. What he didn't know was how he was supposed to convince Papa Teng that he was an honorable man.

"Will you help?" she asked hopefully.

"It depends."

She lowered her head and he watched as her hands went to her robe and opened it. Before he could stop her she had opened the gown beneath it and was showing him her breasts. They were beautiful, full and round with dark brown nipples.

"I can only pay you with—"

"Mrs. Teng," he said, leaning forward and closing her clothes over her breasts, "that is not necessary. That will never be necessary. If I help you it will be because I wish to repay you and your family for saving my life, and that's all."

"I am ashamed now . . ." she said, rising.

"Don't be. What you did took courage, and I admire you for it. To be willing to do . . . that for your family makes you a very special woman."

She buttoned herself and said, "Thank you, Mr. Adams. I believe you are truly a man of honor."

"Now we have only to convince your husband."

"Yes."

"Go back to bed, Mrs. Teng. I will talk with your husband in the morning."

"Thank you." She walked to the door and said, "Good night, Mr. Adams," before going through it without waiting for a reply.

Clint settled back in the bed and knew that he'd gone and done it again. He'd gotten himself involved in someone else's trouble, with the odds stacked against him.

He was getting too old for this.

He went to sleep and dreamed that instead of rejecting Soong Teng's offer, he had taken her to his bed.

ELEVEN

Steve Landergott turned the dark-haired whore over onto her belly and stared at her wide buttocks. He gave one of them a sharp slap, causing the whore to squeal, and told her, "Get up on your knees."

She obeyed, and thrust her buttocks at him. On the right one the red imprint of his hand looked back at him.

He got to his knees behind her, took hold of her hips and slid his cock between her thighs and up into her soaking cunt from behind.

"Oh yeah, baby," the whore said, "that's great, you've got the best—"

"Shut up," he said, slapping her on the rump again. "I don't need any of your whore talk!"

Thereafter the whore kept her mouth shut, except to moan and groan when he thrust himself into her. Landergott knew she was acting but he didn't care. All he was after here was his own physical satisfaction, and he didn't care what she felt—if anything.

He drove himself into her brutally, imagining that she was Papa Teng's wife, or his daughter. Landergott didn't really care which one he got. All he knew was that he wanted one of them slant-eyed gals more than he'd ever wanted another woman. Hell, if he got lucky, after killing the old man and getting the gold he could have both of them gals.

Sometimes he thought he wanted the older one more, because she was sure to be more experienced than the younger one—even if she wasn't getting anything from the old man.

Then sometimes he felt maybe he'd like the younger one because she'd be so tender and sweet, and he could teach her to do the things he liked.

He stopped thinking then because he felt the rush building up inside of him. He increased his speed until finally he was coming, groaning out loud as he filled up the whore's cunt.

When he pulled out of her she rolled over onto her back, displaying big, sloppy breasts and a painfully plain face that was not aging well. If she wasn't forty she was damn close to it.

"How was that, lover?" she asked.

He slapped her face then, a hard, open-handed slap that jarred her and reddened her face.

"I told you I didn't want any of your whore talk!"

"Then gimme my money and get out, you bastard!" she snapped, rubbing her cheek. "I didn't bring you up here to get beat up, and I don't have to take that from anybody, least of all you."

He was going to hit her again when he thought better of it. He got up and pulled his pants up. They had been gathered around his ankles and he hadn't even bothered to kick them away. All he'd wanted from this whore was a quick roll to satisfy his itch. She was hardly the best that the town of Turner's Basin had to offer, but, then, from what he had seen on the street, she wasn't the worst, either. She had a big behind and that was what he'd been looking for, anyway. At least he hadn't had to look at her face while he fucked her.

"Here's your money, bitch!" he said, tossing some bills her way. They fluttered in the air for a moment and then she snatched them up quickly, before they could hit the ground.

"Next time you get the urge, cowboy, do me a favor—find somebody else."

"Don't worry," he said. "This town has to have better to offer than you."

He strapped on his gun and left her room, hoping that she was at least clean enough so that he wouldn't get a disease, or something.

When Steve Landergott reached the saloon, three of his friends were waiting at a table. The fourth one, Whitey, was still up on the mountain, watching the Tengs.

"You get good and taken care of, Steve?" Cole Weston asked with a grin.

"In a way, yeah." Landergott sat down, grabbed the bottle of whiskey that was on the table, and took a swig from it. "Poorest damned excuse for a whore I ever saw."

"Had me one the other day that wasn't too bad," Johnny Sharpe said, grinning. "Damned if she didn't almost swallow my whole cock."

"That ain't sayin' much," Marty Cort said, "considering how small it is."

Sharpe, barely five feet six, was edgy about his height and was always trying to compensate by bragging about the size of his manhood.

"You wish yours was as big as mine—" Sharpe started, but Cort ignored him and turned his attention to Landergott.

"Too bad this town ain't got a slant-eyed whore, huh, Steve?"

"I got my slant-eyed women picked out already, Marty," Landergott reminded him.

"Hey now," Weston said, "you said you was gonna take one and we got the other one."

"Sure, sure . . ."

"You decided which one you want yet, Steve?" Sharpe asked.

"Not yet."

"I'd sure like that older one," Sharpe said. He was twenty-five and liked older women. Sometimes Landergott thought that Johnny Sharpe was trying to fuck his mother over and over again. Sick bastard!

"You can have her," Cole Weston said. He was forty-five, tall, and good-looking, although his good looks were starting to show the ravages of age. He liked the young ones. "That young one looks just about the right age for me."

"You fellas can have the women," Marty Cort said, "and I'll take the gold."

Landergott leaned over quickly and slapped Cort in the face harder than he'd hit the whore. Cort was a big man, just over six feet and thick throughout, but

Landergott was bigger, six-four and all work-hardened muscle.

"What the fuck—" Cort said, his head snapping back and his hat falling off.

"You're lucky we're in this saloon alone right now," Landergott said in a low, tight voice. "Don't go mentioning that gold out loud again, Marty, you hear?"

"I hear you, Steve, I hear you," Cort said, rubbing his cheek. "You don't need to go hittin' me."

Landergott reached across and pushed Cort's face this time, instead of striking it. It was as close as Landergott got to a friendly gesture.

Actually, Cort and Landergott were pretty good friends. Both of them were in their mid-thirties, and they'd been riding together for almost ten years, on and off. Still, Landergott was in charge, there was never much doubt of that.

"When are we gonna move on these Chinks, Steve?" Cole Weston asked. "It's gettin' colder than a whore's heart, you know."

"I know, but we can't move until Papa Teng finds what we're looking for."

"Looks to me like all he's doing is checking every cave he can find," Sharpe said. "Hell, we can do that."

"I told you before, Junior," Landergott said, "that other slant told Papa Teng something else, something that will nail it down for him. We'd be looking all over this mountain for years. Papa Teng is gonna find that cave for us."

"When?" Sharpe asked, frowning because he didn't like to be called Junior, but was too afraid of Steve Landergott to say so.

"Soon."

Sharpe was about to say something else, but a look from Cort stopped him.

"One of us has got to go up there and spell Whitey," Weston said.

"I'll go," Landergott said.

"You were up there yesterday, Steve," Cort said. "Why not let me go, or Weston—"

"I'll go," Landergott said. He took another swig from the bottle and said, "I'll go and saddle my horse."

As Landergott went out Sharpe whistled softly and said, "Sometimes I think he wants one of them Chinky gals more than he wants the gold."

"If that was the case," Cort said, "we'd just ride up there and take them, wouldn't we?"

"I guess so."

"Don't be fooled, Johnny. Steve wants it all, and he intends to get it. I pity the fool who stands in his way."

TWELVE

In the morning at breakfast Clint could feel the tension in the air again. It didn't help that Soong Teng would not look at him at all, which was noticeable to everyone, especially Papa Teng.

After breakfast Clint dressed and went outside for the first time in days. The cool mountain air felt good on his face, and in his lungs. Papa Teng and his boys had already left, which was just as well. There was less tension when they weren't around. Actually, the tension was probably caused in part by Clint's presence, so it would be lessened when he left there for good.

He went around back to check on Duke and found the big black gelding in fine spirits.

"You like the cold, don't you, big boy?" Clint said, stroking the gelding's massive neck. "Well, it's too bad I hate it. Guess you should have hooked up with someone with a little thicker skin, huh?"

He took Duke out of the shed and walked him around a bit, just to stretch his legs, then brought him back to the shed. Papa Teng had apparently used some grain that he had, and mixed it with some cut-up dried fruit, but Clint knew he'd have to get Duke some proper feed pretty soon.

Along near afternoon he decided to get some exercise himself and chopped some wood for the fireplace. He carried it inside and set it down near the fire, which was constantly going. The house was really little more than a shack split into three rooms. Papa Teng and his wife slept in one, Sooni/Donna in the other one—yes, he'd learned that he was sleeping in Donna's bed—and the boys bunked on the floor in the main room. The cold seemed to go right through the walls, so they needed a constant fire, and at night plenty of blankets.

He found that he was winded from chopping the wood and sat down at the table to take a breather.

Soong Teng entered the room and he felt the tension in the air then, but it was a different kind. Now she wasn't avoiding his face, but was looking directly at him.

And he had seen that look before.

When Landergott reached the place where Whitey's horse was picketed he dismounted and tied off his mount. He pulled the fur collar of his jacket up to cover his neck better and started walking. About forty yards farther up he found Warren "Whitey" Longtree, crouched down, watching the shack where the Tengs were living.

"What's going on, Whitey?"

Longtree was a half-breed, called "Whitey" even though his hair was dark, because he hated the Indian half of himself. He was about five eight but powerfully built. Indeed, of the four men he rode with, Landergott felt that only Whitey could match his own strength—nearly.

"Nothing much. That fella they drug home is still inside."

"Guess he didn't freeze to death then, huh?"

"I guess not. Came out a little while ago and chopped some wood."

"Well, if he wants to stay alive he'd better up and leave, pronto."

"Before they find the gold, anyways," Whitey Longtree said.

"Yeah. Why don't you head down to town, Whitey, get yourself a woman or something."

"A drink first, then a hot meal, and then a woman," Whitey said. "See you."

"Yeah."

As Whitey left, Landergott found himself a comfortable position on the snow-packed ground and lit a cigarillo. He held it cupped in his hand and blew the smoke down toward the ground, so he wouldn't be spotted by accident from the house.

He thought about working on the railroad with the Chinks and hearing them talk about gold one day when they didn't know he was close enough to hear. He remembered trying to beat the location out of Khan and then suddenly snapping the man's neck like a twig, and just by accident. The damned Chink was so small and brittle that he just broke in Landergott's hands. That was when he decided that he was going to have to play it smart from there on. He trailed the Chinks when they left, knowing that they would lead him to the gold.

He remembered hot days when he was working the railroad, and he would see Papa Teng's wife and daughter with their sweaty clothes stuck to their bodies. Jesus, you could even see their teats—that is, until the crew leader made them start wearing bigger, looser clothes. Just thinking about those Chink gals was giving him an erection again. Couldn't think straight when that happened. He pulled his dick out into the cold, jerked on it dispassionately until he shot his load right there in the snow, where it lay steaming.

Plenty more where that came from, Chinky gals, plenty more.

THIRTEEN

Soong Teng was moving about the room now, cleaning—or pretending to clean. Clint felt that he should stand up and leave the room, but it would have been very conspicuous for him to do so.

Donna came out of her room, now, and Clint felt grateful for her presence.

"I am going to go out for a walk, Mama."

"I do not like you walking alone, Sooni."

"I will be fine. I want to find some pinecones so we can throw them into the fire. The house will smell better that way, don't you think, Clint?"

"That's a fine idea, Donna. Maybe I'll come along with you."

He started to rise, but she put her hands on his shoulders and said, "No, you must rest. I saw you chopping wood and you must be tired. I won't be gone very long. Perhaps half an hour or so."

When she left, Soong Teng looked at Clint and said,

"She always says that, and then she is gone for an hour."

"I guess she loses track of time," he said. Damn, but he felt nervous, because she was looking at him the way a woman looks at a man she wants.

She put down the rag she had been using and dropped any pretense of cleaning.

"Clint, I must talk to you again."

"Did you tell Papa yet about our talk last night?"

"No, not yet. I will tell him tonight. What I want to talk to you about now is . . . is something else, and I must say it quickly, because we haven't much time."

"Soong—"

"Clint, I want you to love me."

Steve Landergott perked up when he saw the younger Chinese girl leave the house. What was her name? Donna, she wanted to be called. He'd talked to her some when they were working the railroad, and he could tell that he frightened her. That excited him.

He decided to follow her.

"Soong Teng—" Clint said.

"No, that is wrong," she said, clasping her hands. "I want you to make love to me—yes, that is correct."

"No, it's not—"

"Yes, it is," she said, looking puzzled.

"No, I mean it's right, but it's not . . . proper . . ."

She was moving across the room toward him, and he suddenly noticed that her hair was down. He hadn't seen her take it down. It was long and silky-looking, fine and very, very black . . .

"I was nineteen when Sooni was born, Clint," she

explained. Doing some quick mental math he figured her to be about thirty-seven or -eight. "My husband is sixty-two years old. Ours was an arranged marriage, and it was good . . . for a while. For the past three years Papa has been unable to . . . to be a man with me in bed. Do you understand?"

"Yes."

"He is still my husband and I honor him," she said—and he noticed that her dress was unbuttoned, "but I have needs that he cannot satisfy, and I ask you . . . please . . ."

She dropped her dress to the ground and there she was, naked, the cold causing her nipples to pucker. She was exquisitely formed, like a doll, but her breasts were larger than one might have expected.

"Soong, if Sooni . . . Donna . . . comes back . . ."

"She will be gone for an hour," Soong Teng said, "and Papa and the boys will not be back until this evening."

"Soong—" he said as she came up close enough to him for him to feel the heat of her body. There was also a great heat in his crotch . . .

"Clint . . ."

She was on him, then, sitting on his lap, her arms around his neck, her breasts in his face, and he was beyond resisting.

It would be so easy, Landergott thought. Just run up behind her, grab her, tear off her clothes, throw her on the ground, on the snow, drop his pants and ram it into her . . .

Jesus, but he was hard again!

He could feel her heat right through his clothes as

she squirmed in his lap. His mouth was on her breasts, sucking her nipples, biting her flesh gently so as not to leave any marks. Did Papa Teng even see her naked anymore?

She moaned as he bit her nipples and she pulled his head up so she could kiss him, her tongue sliding into his mouth. She was on fire with need, he could feel it, like the fire that was in the fireplace . . .

He reached down and cupped his hand over her pubic mound. It was already wet, and he slipped a finger into her. Quickly, she came, a small, fleeting orgasm that left her breathless, nevertheless . . .

She started to speak in Chinese, into his ear as he kissed her throat, her breasts, ran his other hand over her back, down to the swell of her buttocks. He moved his finger inside her and she gasped.

"Please . . ." she said, "please . . ."

He stood up, sweeping her into his arms. He stood there, undecided about where to take her. To the bed she shared with her husband? To her daughter's bed?

Where?

Landergott followed the girl at a safe distance, watching as she picked things up off the ground, some of which she examined and discarded, and some of which she kept.

There was no one else around, he knew. They were even far enough away from the house that no one would hear her if she screamed.

It was tempting, very tempting . . .

"The floor," she said, biting his ear, breathing into it, "I don't care . . . on the floor . . ."

He put her down on her feet and went to get a

blanket, which he spread on the floor. Her eyes swept over him hungrily as he undressed, and when his erection sprang free she grabbed for it, fell to her knees, and began to kiss it, murmuring to it in Chinese. She took it into her mouth and sucked it wetly. Briefly, he wondered how a woman who had not had sex for three years could be so expert—but then she hadn't said that she'd been without sex for three years, just that she and Papa Teng hadn't had sex for that period of time. Of course, there had been others, then, others who helped her when the need came . . .

She fondled his balls and suckled him and all thoughts fled from his mind. At that moment he didn't care how many others there had been, just that he was there now, and that was what counted . . .

He filled his hands with her hair as she continued to suckle him, and as he was nearing the point of orgasm she let him slide free from her mouth and laid down on her back on the blanket. There were other things he wanted to do with her, but his cock was covered with her saliva and was so cold with the air hitting it that he immediately sought the safety of her cunt. He slammed into her forcefully, bringing a gasp from her lips, and he moaned as the heat of her surrounded him. He began to drive into her then, in and out, and she wrapped her legs around him and clutched at him, gasping and moaning and meeting his every thrust until finally they both achieved orgasm together . . .

When Donna returned forty minutes later, Clint and her mother had just gotten their clothes back on and the blanket off the floor. It had been that close.

They had sat and talked after the first time, both admitting their feelings of guilt, and then they had made love a second time, and Clint did more of the things he'd wanted to do, and Soong had loved them all. In the midst of a shattering orgasm she had thanked him over and over. The woman was simply incredible for a man's ego, making him feel like a god who had bestowed some great gift upon her.

When Donna walked in, both of them were careful not to look at each other—perhaps overly careful, but Donna was so bright and cheery, talking about the pinecones she'd collected and the rabbit she'd seen, that she didn't notice anything.

Clint swore to himself that it wouldn't happen again, no matter what. Then he looked at Soong Teng and felt himself growing hard again.

Landergott was back in his former position, watching the house. He had resisted his urges and had simply followed the young Chinese girl back to the house. It would all be better when he had the women *and* the gold.

When he had it all!

FOURTEEN

"Is there a town near here?"

It was such a natural question that Clint was surprised that he had not asked it before then.

"Yes," Papa Teng said, "about three miles south is the town of Turner's Basin."

"It is so small, it is hardly a town," Ling offered.

"Ling has gone there with Papa and I have not," Chang said. It sounded to Clint like an old complaint. "If you are going to go there, Clint—uh, Mr. Adams, would you take me with you?"

"That would be up to your father, Chang," Clint said carefully, "if I go."

"Why would you go?" Donna asked.

"Well, for one thing it would have a hotel where I could stay instead of imposing on you and your family."

"You are not imposing, Clint, is he, Papa?" she asked her father.

"We have little, but what we have it is our honor

to share," Papa Teng said—it was the way in which he said it, though, which sounded to Clint as if Papa was saying, "Yes, he is imposing."

"Also, if my rig is damaged they might have a blacksmith's shop."

"We could go in and check," Chang said, and that drew a glare from Papa Teng. In fact, Papa Teng seemed to have little more than a glare for everyone in his family.

For a moment it occurred to Clint that Papa Teng had arrived home early and had seen his wife and Clint on the floor of the cabin—but no, that was looking for more trouble than he already had.

Then he wondered if Soong Teng had told Papa yet about their talk.

"First I'd have to check my rig. Papa Teng, could one of the boys show me where it is?"

Papa Teng looked at both of his boys and silenced them before they could start shouting.

"Ling can take you there."

Ling gave his younger brother a superior look and said to Clint, "When would you like to go?"

"First thing in the morning, I guess. The sooner I check it out the sooner whatever's broken gets fixed."

After dinner Donna helped her mother with the dishes and Ling and Chang went out to check on Duke.

That left Papa Teng and Clint at the table, Papa with tea and Clint with a cup of coffee.

"Papa—"

"My wife has already told me about your conversation last night," Papa Teng said, as if he were a mind reader.

"I see."

"She should not have said anything."

"But she did. Papa Teng, if there is anything I can do to help, to repay your kindness—"

"I do not barter for favors," Papa Teng said. "I do what I do out of honor, and honor does not need to be repaid."

"With all due respect, Papa, in my culture a favor rates the return of a favor. That's how it's done in this country. I would always feel indebted to you if I'm not able to return the favor."

Papa Teng seemed to consider that and then abruptly changed the subject.

"If you need to go into town I will accompany you. We need some more supplies."

"All right," Clint said, giving in for now. Maybe during a trip into town he could work on the stubborn Chinaman some more.

As everyone was getting ready for bed, Clint offered to give Donna back her bed, and she refused.

"You can use it for one more night."

"Where have you been sleeping?"

"Out here with my brothers. It is all right, Papa hangs a blanket for me."

"I really appreciate everything your family has done, Donna—especially you. Giving me your bed, nursing me back to health—"

"I am happy to do it, Clint, truly. I have to tell you something though."

"What?"

She looked back, to see if either of her brothers were listening.

"I do not look forward to the day you will be leaving."

"That's very nice of you to say, Donna."

She smiled at him, and suddenly he was aware of the look in her eyes, that look again. Donna, at eighteen, was definitely a woman, and she was giving him that look that women had.

Suddenly, Clint *was* looking forward to the day he would leave, but he felt that it was probably farther off than any of them imagined.

As the lights went out in the house Landergott got up to leave. It was too damned cold to stay there all night and watch the house, and he didn't think the Tengs would be leaving in the middle of the night, anyway.

First thing he was going to do when he got bac'k to town was find a dark-haired whore.

During the night Clint became aware of a presence in his room. From the smell, it was a female presence. God, he thought, Soong can't possibly think of repeating what they had done that afternoon, right under everyone's noses.

He reached for the lamp, turned it up, and said, "Soon—" and stopped short when he saw who it was.

It was not Soong, but her daughter, Sooni—or Donna.

"How did you know it was me before you turned up the light?" she asked.

Obviously, she thought he was going to say "Sooni," as he'd started to say "Soong,"—which was very lucky, indeed.

"I could smell you."

"Oh," she said, and he thought that she was pleased with the answer.

"Donna, what are you doing here?"

"I am afraid."

"Of what?"

"That your wagon will not be damaged, and that somehow you will leave tomorrow."

"Donna—"

"That would mean that this is the last night you will be here."

"Donna—"

"And I don't want you to leave without telling you that I—I have feelings for you."

"Donna, I don't think—"

"I am eighteen, Clint," she said, sitting on the bed. "I am a woman."

"I know that, and you're a very lovely woman—"

"You have said that before, which is how I know you like me—and I like you, Clint, very, very much."

"I'm flattered—"

"Kiss me, please?"

"Donna—"

"Just a kiss? That will not hurt, will it?"

No, he thought, but it could definitely lead to other things.

He kissed her, intending it to be a gentle kiss, and it was, but it still wasn't the kind of kiss he'd intended it to be. It was the most passionate gentle kiss he'd ever experienced. She opened her mouth easily, and he opened his, and the kiss just went on and on. She moaned once, deep in her throat, and then reached for him, sliding her hand inside his long johns to touch his chest. Suddenly, he felt himself sliding her night-gown up and easing his hand beneath it. Her skin was soft and hot as his hands traveled up her belly to her breasts. They were smaller than her mother's, but no less firm, with the same large nipples. He rubbed his palms over her nipples in a slow, circular motion and her hand closed over the hair on his chest, tugging at it.

"Donna—" he said, sliding his mouth away from hers. God, she had a sweet mouth! "Donna, we can't—"

"Why not?" she asked, her eyes shining, her lips swollen. "I want you, Clint—"

"Not here—"

"Yes, here," she said with sudden fervor. "Clint, if you do not make love to me here, I will—will cry out for my father."

"Donna!"

"I will," she said fiercely, yanking on the hair of his chest painfully.

He studied her determined face and saw that she meant what she said.

"Jesus—" he said, and kissed her again.

He closed his hands over her breasts and thumbed her nipples. Her breasts did not fill his hands as fully as her mother's had, but somehow her skin was smoother.

She slid her other hand into his long johns and slid them down to his waist. He lifted his hips so she could slide them off, and then her hands were on his cock, as if it were some secret treasure she had just discovered. She licked it, sucked it, squeezed it, and then moved up so that he could suck her breasts and hold her tight.

They moved on the bed so that she was on the bottom, and Clint slid her nightgown over her head and dropped it to the floor. Her nipples were dark brown, like her mother's. He raised himself over her and she grabbed his hips and guided him until his cock was pushing against the wet lips of her puss.

With one movement he entered her, easily and fully. She smiled, then laughed softly in his ear as he began to ride her, easily so that there would be no noise.

She came first. In spite of the fact that she was biting her lower lips to keep silent, to him she seemed to make a lot of noise. He half expected to be discovered at any moment, as he had that afternoon with her mother. In either case, if discovered, how would he prove himself an honorable man, then.

His orgasm followed seconds later, and he stopped thinking. If the rest of the family had entered the room at that precise moment, he wouldn't have noticed them. All he knew was the feel of her warm insides, sucking at him, pulling his seed from him almost painfully. She laughed again as he filled her up, sliding her hands down over his buttocks and stroking them while he emptied himself.

It was over almost as it had begun, but she seemed to be satisfied. He certainly was! So much so that he wished they had more time.

"That was beautiful," she said, "very beautiful." She kissed him fleetingly and said, "Now I know you won't leave tomorrow."

"How do you know that?"

"I just do."

She left the room quietly then and he turned the lamp down and did not bother donning his long johns again. The bed still held her incredible warmth.

It was only as he was falling asleep that he realized she wasn't a virgin. Not by a long sight!

FIFTEEN

In the morning breakfast was, to say the least, interesting. Both Soong and Donna averted their eyes when Clint looked at them, and Papa Teng never took his eyes from the plate. Only the two boys, Ling and Chang, ate and chattered as they always did.

After breakfast Clint and Ling left to go and examine Clint's rig. Ling knew exactly where it was, which impressed Clint. He wasn't sure he'd even be able to get back to the house without the boy.

When they reached it Clint could see the tracks of his team around the rig, even though they were almost completely obliterated.

"We looks for your horses, Mr. Adams, but we were not able to find them."

"I can always get a new team," Clint said. The loss of the horses was unfortunate, but not the blow that losing Duke would have been. "And when we're not around your father, Ling, you can call me Clint. I won't consider it a lack of respect. In fact, I'd consider it a sign that we are friends."

"All right, Clint!" the boy said, using the first name enthusiastically.

"Well, let's get a look at this rig."

Ling watched as Clint crawled over the rig, checked underneath and inside.

"How is it?"

"Just what I was afraid of," Clint said, wiping his hands together. "The axle is broken. Not only will I need a blacksmith's shop, I'll need the blacksmith to come out here and repair it."

"Should we go back now?"

"Yes. It's still early enough to go to town. Let me get some things out of the back, first."

Clint went into the rig. He'd noticed before that everything was a mess. The force of the rig falling over had jarred everything loose that had been hanging on the walls. He picked through everything, but could not find much that he considered of real value. The only thing he took was the .22 Colt New Line, and a Winchester. If he ended up helping the Tengs against Landergott and the others, he could always go back to the rig for more firepower.

"All right, let's get back to the house."

When they reached the house Papa Teng and Chang were getting ready to go to town.

"We weren't sure you would get back in time," Papa Teng said.

"Well, we're back," Clint said. "How do you get to town, Papa?"

"We walk."

"Walk. What about a wagon, or a buggy? You must have used something to get here with?"

"We had to trade the wagon for supplies."

"And now? What will you use for supplies now?"

"We have a few things left to trade with."

"And when you run out of things to trade?"

For the first time since they'd met he noticed a sign of uncertainty in the old Chinaman.

"I . . . do not know."

"Papa Teng, eventually you'll have to give up searching for the gold."

Papa Teng threw him a quick look and Clint was able to read it. Papa Teng was thinking that Clint might be trying to talk him out of looking so that he could look for the gold himself.

"Relax, Papa. I'm not interested in your gold, just the welfare of your family."

"Which is exactly what I am interested in, Mr. Adams."

"Yeah, I guess so. We'll take my horse, Papa, and use my money for supplies."

Papa gave him a stern look. "I am not interested in your charity."

"Don't be so stubborn, Papa. I'm only trying to give back some of what you and your family have given me."

They exchanged stares, and then Papa Teng nodded.

Clint saddled Duke and got Papa and Chang up on his back. When they came back, depending on the amount of supplies they purchased, one or both of them might have to walk.

Soong Teng and Donna watched from the door and waved. It occurred to Clint that someone should stay behind with them, but then whatever Landergott wanted would come from Papa, and not the rest of his family. As much as the man might want one of the women, he'd want the gold more.

Clint was sure of that.

Johnny Sharpe watched as the old man and the stranger left with the two kids. That left the two women behind.

Boy, that young one sure looked sweet.

SIXTEEN

Turner's Basin wasn't much of a town. It was actually located inside a small basinlike depression. Clint wondered what would happen if it ever rained for forty days and forty nights.

At least it had a blacksmith.

"Go where?" the man asked. He had the prerequisite blacksmith's set of shoulders, and the beginnings of a solid paunch to go with it.

"It's just four or five miles outside of town. My axle needs repairing."

"Mister, if your axle is busted, what you need is a new axle. That means I got to lug it out there with me and make the repairs under adverse conditions."

The man sounded too educated to be stuck in a nothing town like Turner's Basin.

"I'll pay you for the travel time."

"Travel time is expensive."

"I can carry the weight."

The man studied Clint for a few moments, then said, "Show me."

Clint took out twenty dollars and dropped it on the ground in front of the man.

"Why you—" the man said, swinging a massive right fist.

Clint ducked under the blow and pushed his right foot between the man's legs at the ankles. The blacksmith got tangled up and ended up on his ass next to the twenty dollars. Clint hoped he wouldn't get up. After all the time he'd spent in bed lately he didn't think he could go a couple of rounds with this bruiser.

"While you're down there you can pick up the twenty dollars," he suggested.

The man did so, then stood up and faced Clint, who stood ready.

"The name's Stoneman, Horace Stoneman."

"I'll bet people call you Stoney."

"Gee, you're quick," the man said sarcastically. "Be ready to leave in an hour."

"I'll be ready."

Clint went over to the general store and found Papa Teng having an argument with the clerk behind the desk.

"Now I told you, Chinaman, I won't settle for nothing but cash."

Clint walked in and Papa Teng saw him.

"The gentleman does not believe that I can pay cash."

Clint took out five dollars this time and put it on the counter in front of the man.

"We've got cash."

"You with them?"

"I am."

The man shrugged, picked up the five dollars and Papa's list.

"This'll do for a start," he said to Clint, about the five dollars.

"There's more. Just tally it up and have it ready to load."

Clint walked outside with Papa Teng and the boys in tow.

"What is he going to load the supplies on?" Papa asked.

"A wagon. The blacksmith is coming with us and we'll use his wagon."

"He has agreed?"

"He will."

Clint spotted the saloon down the street.

"Listen, Papa, why don't you wait here with the boys. I'm going to go and get a drink."

"All right."

"Come over here," Landergott called out to Marty Cort, with whom he was sharing the hotel room.

Cort went over to the window and looked out.

"You see what I see?"

"Yeah," Cort said. "A Chinaman and two Chinese kids."

"That's not just any Chinaman, Marty. That's Papa Teng himself."

"The Chinaman with the gold?"

"Yep."

Landergott had been the only one working on the railroad crew. Things had gotten slow and he'd taken the job until something better came along. Papa Teng was that something, and he'd brought the others in on it.

Of course, he and Marty Cort had no intention of sharing the gold with the others.

And he had no intention of sharing it with Marty Cort.

"What's he doing in town?" Cort asked.

"Probably came in for supplies."

"Why don't we go down and ask him how the search is going?"

"Sure, show ourselves to him now and he'd take off."

"Not while the gold is still around."

"He'd change location, then."

"We'd find him."

Landergott looked at Cort and said, "Marty, we're going to do this my way. Got it?"

"Sure, Steve. Don't we always do things your way?"

"Yeah, Marty, we do. Don't forget that."

"Just don't forget that gold is getting split at least two ways. Okay?"

"Sure, didn't I say it was?"

"Yeah," Cort said, going back to sit on the bed. "You said."

Landergott stared out the window down at Papa Teng. He wondered if he could get the old man to talk, cutting into the waiting time.

There might be a way.

Johnny Sharpe couldn't wait any longer.

All he'd heard so far was *talk* about gold, and *talk* about the women. Well, the women were here now for the taking.

And Johnny Sharpe was ready to take.

• • •

Clint walked over to the saloon, which was empty that early in the day. He went to the bar and ordered a drink.

"Pretty quiet town," he said to the bartender, a bored-looking man in his fifties.

"What's not to be quiet? Place is out in the middle of nowhere."

"Yeah, I noticed. Guess you don't get too many strangers in town."

"More than you'd think."

"Yeah?"

"You, for instance."

"Rig broke down outside of town. As soon as I can get it fixed I'm on my way."

"You'd think most strangers would come to this town for that reason."

"Why? You got some here who aren't in a hurry to leave?"

"Five."

"No kidding?"

"They just sit in here all afternoon into the evening and drink and wait."

"For what?"

"Who knows, but only four of them come in here. I don't know what the other one does."

"The same four?"

"Nope. There's always somebody different missing."

"You notice a lot."

"Not much else to do."

"I guess not. What do these fellas look like?"

The bartender's eyes suddenly got suspicious.

"Why you asking?"

Clint shrugged.

"Not much else to do while I'm waiting for the blacksmith. Forget I asked."

"They're pretty ordinary-looking—except for one."

"Oh, yeah?"

"Big man, blond, with a scar that almost closes one eye. Ugly bruiser."

Landergott! And judging from what the bartender had to say, he had four men with him for help—and one of them was watching the Tengs at all times.

And both women were alone!

SEVENTEEN

Neither Soong nor Donna heard the man when he entered. The door had been closed, but it opened soundlessly, and suddenly he was standing there.

At first they were not afraid. He was a small man, and did not look dangerous, but then Soong saw his eyes. She had seen eyes like that before since coming to this country from China. She knew that many men saw Chinese women as desirable, because they looked different. She had experienced this in places like San Francisco and Sacramento, and even when Papa Teng worked on the railroad crew.

Now she saw it again.

"What do you want?"

"That's a silly question, isn't it?" the man asked. "I want you."

Soong saw that he was a very young man, not much older than her Sooni.

"Let my daughter go," Soong Teng said. "I will do what you want."

"Mama—"

"Hush."

"Well now," the man said, a cocky grin on his face now. "I don't rightly know which one I want," he drawled, and then added, "first."

"I didn't agree to haul no—" the blacksmith started to complain, but Clint was already loading the supplies onto the wagon.

"The boys can ride in the back, and you, Papa Teng, up front with the blacksmith."

"Hey, now wait a minute—"

"Shut up, Stoney. You'll get paid extra, don't worry."

"I just want what I deserve."

"If I paid you that little—ah, never mind."

Clint mounted Duke and Stoneman said, "Where are you going?"

"I'm riding up ahead. They'll show you where my rig is and you can get started."

"Hey!" Stoneman shouted, but Clint was already gone, riding hell-bent for leather. "Where is he going in such a hurry?"

Papa Teng was staring after Clint and said, "I do not know."

"That stranger sure is heading out fast," Landergott said.

"Where to, do you think? Leaving?"

"Naw, I think he's heading back to the shack—and in a hurry!"

"Why?"

"Because those two women are alone up there."

"So?"

"You know Johnny. He gets impatient sometimes."

"Sure, you know Johnny and I know Johnny, but how does he know— Come on," Landergott said abruptly, heading for the door.

"Where to?"

"The saloon," Landergott said. "I want to see what that stranger found out that made him leave town in such an all-fired hurry."

Damn, Johnny Sharpe thought, this China gal sure had the softest, juiciest box he'd ever poked.

He was standing behind Soong Teng, who was naked and leaning on the wooden table, her behind hiked into the air. Johnny Sharpe had his pants down around his ankles and his shaft was buried in Soong Teng's cunt. Donna was watching from a corner of the room, helpless to aid her mother because the man had his gun in his right hand. He was running his left hand over Soong Teng's sweaty back and moving his hips back and forth. Every time his crotch banged into her firm buttocks and his dick drove deep inside of her, he closed his eyes and bit his lip.

He'd made the right choice, he knew he did. The older woman was the one he'd wanted all along, and even though the younger one looked sweeter than candy he knew he'd made the right choice when he told the older one to strip. She had great breasts and when he made her turn around so he could examine her his dick had gotten rock-hard when he saw her ass.

"Come on, China gal," he'd told her, "bend over

this here table. Johnny's got something good for you."

"You won't hurt my daughter?" the older woman had asked.

"Not if you give me what I want. Hell, I might even give her the same thing I give you. She might want it by the time she finishes watching."

Now Donna watched and saw that the man closed his eyes every time he brought his hips forward. She saw her mother's face contorted, her eyes squeezed shut, and felt her mother's shame as if it were her own. The man grabbed Soong Teng's hair in his left hand and pulled so that her head was pulled back painfully, but he was oblivious to anything but his own pleasure.

She wondered if she'd have time to rush the man before he saw her and shot her.

She was about to try when the door slammed open and Clint Adams stood in the doorway.

The man with the gun looked at the door, exclaiming, "What the—"

He brought his gun up when he saw Clint, but he was too slow. Donna saw Clint's gun appear in his hand, and she hadn't even seen him draw it. He fired, and the bullet struck the man in the forehead.

Just as the bullet struck, Johnny felt himself coming in the China gal's cunt.

Jesus, he thought, what a way to die.

Soong Teng screamed.

EIGHTEEN

Clint came back after burying the man behind the house.

Soong Teng was calm now, almost frighteningly calm. He could imagine how she must have felt with a dead man's seed pumping into her.

She was seated at the table with Donna now—the same table she'd bent over when he first opened the door.

"Soong Teng—"

"Papa Teng must not know," she said firmly.

"Soong—"

"Clint," she said, looking at him now, "it would serve no purpose to tell him."

"He has to know that the man was here, that Landergott's in town."

"That man worked for Landergott?" Donna asked.

"Yes, and he's in town with three more."

"What was this man doing?" Donna asked.

"Watching. They all take turns watching. Apparently, this man got impatient and took advantage of the fact that you were both alone. Did he ask about the gold?"

"No," Donna said.

"That's strange."

"Clint—" Soong said, and he walked to the table and took her hand. He felt her flinch when he touched her and pulled his hand away. Donna looked at them both and suddenly became aware that there was something between them—but what?

"Please," Soong said, looking at Clint and then at Donna, "Papa must not know."

"Donna?" Clint said.

She looked at Clint, and then nodded, squeezing her mother's other hand.

"Soong Teng," Clint said. He crouched down next to her and took her hand. She flinched again when he touched her, but he held her tightly. "Papa will know something is wrong if you pull away from his touch."

Soong looked at Clint, her eyes haunted for a moment longer, and then she smiled and squeezed his hand back.

"I will not pull away. After all, the man did not do anything to me I have not done before with . . . with other men."

"Yes, he did. He did it violently, and that is the horror of it."

"I will survive."

"I know you will," Clint said, standing up. "I have to go to my wagon and make sure it's repaired. Papa and the boys will be coming back. I will tell them . . .

what we want them to know about what happened here."

"All right."

He took a moment to get the story straight with them, and then said to Soong Teng, "Talk to Donna, Soong Teng. She is the only one right now who might be able to understand what you went through. She can help you get over it."

"Yes," Soong Teng said, squeezing her daughter's hand, "she is a woman now."

Donna put her head on her mother's shoulder, and Clint left them that way.

When Clint reached his rig, Stoney the blacksmith was already at work. He drew Papa Teng off to one side and explained what had happened, leaving out the rape aspect. He also explained about Landergott and his cronies.

Papa Teng listened stonily and then said, "I am indebted to you for saving my wife and daughter."

"That in no way repays the debt I owe you, Papa. When we get back to the house I'd like to talk to you about helping you with Landergott."

"Yes," Papa said after a moment, "perhaps it is time to talk of that."

"Go back to the house, Papa. Leave the boys with me, if you like."

"No, I will take them. Our family must be together when we talk. Later, you and I will talk."

"All right."

Papa went and got the boys, and they left Clint and Stoney tending to the rig.

Clint went over to Stoney and said, "There was

something else I wanted to ask you about."

"Yeah, what?"

"Do you have any horses for sale?"

Stoney looked over at him and said, "You want a helluva lot, don't you, friend?"

"Only what I pay for."

NINETEEN

Landergott got what he wanted out of the bartender, and then let the man fall to the floor. He'd had to do little more than show the man his strength by grabbing the front of his shirt and lifting him off the floor.

"Get us some drinks."

"Sure, mister, sure."

On the way out of the hotel Landergott and Cort had stopped for the other two men, Weston and Longtree. Now they all sat at a table together.

"What's going on, Landergott?" Weston asked.

"It looks like the Chinaman might know we're around."

"How'd that happen?"

"The stranger. He found out about us from the bartender and lit out of here."

"What about Johnny?" Weston asked.

"Johnny can take care of himself."

"Then should I go up and relieve him as planned?" Weston asked.

"I don't think so," Landergott said. "We agreed in advance that if a man didn't come and relieve one of us, that one would come back to town. We'll wait and see if Johnny comes back down."

"And then what?"

"If he doesn't, then we'll all go up."

"This thing's gone bad, hasn't it?" Weston asked. "Because of the stranger."

"Too bad we don't know who he is," Longtree said.

"Maybe we can find out," Landergott said.

"How?"

"From the blacksmith, when he comes back."

"Well, at least one thing good has come of this," Cort said.

"What's that?" Landergott asked.

"The waiting is over."

"Oh, yes," Landergott said, "the waiting is definitely over."

TWENTY

It was late in the day before the rig was repaired and ready to be righted.

"We'll need some help to get this thing up."

"What help?" Stoney asked. "There's two of us, isn't there?"

"Yeah, but—"

"Grab yourself a good tree limb to use as leverage," Stoney told him.

Clint went and found a six-foot-long hunk of tree limb that was thick enough to use for leverage and a hatchet from the back of his rig to cut it down. As he was returning to the wagon he noticed something for the first time. There were tracks in the snow near the wagon. They looked like the tracks of a huge dog—or a wolf.

When he returned to the rig Stoney had moved a large boulder over to it, so that Clint could use it with the tree limb to lever the rig up off its side.

"How'd you move that boulder?" Clint asked.

"It isn't anything but a little pebble," Stoney said. "I carried it."

Clint put his foot against the boulder and pushed, but was unable to move it. How the hell had the blacksmith been able to carry it by himself? The man's strength must have been phenomenal.

"Stoney, are there any wolves in this area?"

"Not wolves . . ."

"Oh."

". . . just one. A huge, shaggy gray."

"Wonderful. Just what I need to make my day complete."

"Shall we get this rig raised?"

"Why not?"

Clint wedged the limb underneath the rig and watched as Stoney moved to the other end of the wagon and grabbed on, his solid hands full of wood.

"All right," he said, "on three we lift. Ready?"

"I'm ready, but I don't—"

"One . . . two . . . three . . ."

Before he could even put his shoulder into the tree limb Clint felt the wagon move off the ground. The man's strength was incredible. Clint hurried to bring the branch up and take his share of the weight, but all during the righting process he felt that Stoney was taking more than his share. At one point he looked over at the blacksmith and saw that, in spite of the weather, the man was sweating—and smiling!

Abruptly, the wagon came down on its wheels and Clint released the branch. He looked over at the blacksmith, who was down on one knee, apparently in some sort of physical distress.

"Are you all right?" Clint asked, rushing to the man's aid.

"I'm fine," Horace Stoneman gasped. "Just not as young as I used to be."

With that the man stood up and said, "You got my money?"

"Sure, I've got your money," Clint said, but in his own mind he was thinking that maybe—just maybe—he had something else he hadn't counted on.

Maybe *he* had help in helping Papa Teng.

Clint convinced Stoneman to accompany him to Papa Teng's house for something to drink and eat. When they arrived it was clear that there had been a family meeting, only Clint couldn't quite read what the outcome might have been.

When Stoney was seated at the table eating with both hands, Clint pulled Papa Teng over to the side.

"I know I may be overstepping my bounds here, Papa, but if you agree to let me help you, I think we could use this man on our side. His strength is incredible."

"Can he shoot a gun?"

"I don't know, but I witnessed a feat of strength that *had* to be seen to be believed. I think if we can get him on our side—that is, if I am on 'our' side."

"I think, Mr. Adams, we should talk about what you want—"

"I don't want anything."

"Then, what do you want for your friend?"

Clint looked at Stoney and saw a mountain of a man shoveling food in enthusiastically with both hands. What *would* a man like that want to help?

"Some of the gold?"

Clint looked at Papa Teng and said, "We'd have to tell him about the gold—but before we could do that I'd have to know about it myself."

"Perhaps, then, we should talk first."

"Yes," Clint agreed, "I guess I was getting ahead of myself. Let me pay him off and send him back to town, and then we can talk."

"Very well."

Clint went to the table, had something to eat with Stoney, and then settled up with him.

"If you need some more work done," Stoney said before he left, "do me a favor—bring it to town."

"If I can. Can you tell me something?"

"What?"

"Is there a sheriff in town?"

"You might say that."

"Why might?"

"We've got a man who walks around wearing a badge. In that regard, he's a sheriff."

"Okay. Thanks for your help, Stoney."

"Don't thank me, you paid for it."

Clint watched the big man drive away in his wagon, and then remembered that he had to talk to him about a team. He'd have to go into town to see him after all. When he thought about the strength of the man, and the size—Jeez, he had to be almost six eight and three hundred pounds, maybe more. He thought back to that moment in town when they'd been on the verge of a scrape and thanked his luck that it hadn't gone further than it had. Papa Teng would be lucky to have Stoney on his side, but the old man was right. They had to decide how much to tell him, and what to offer him. Gold did funny things to people.

He thought briefly about stopping in to see the sheriff in town, but if what Stoney said was true, that would only be a waste of time. He didn't like the idea of not informing the law of a killing, but in this case he made an exception.

He went back into the house to talk to Papa Teng.

Landergott and company got to Papa Teng's in time to see the blacksmith drive away. They had left their horses far enough away so that they wouldn't be heard and walked to the point they had been using to watch the house. Johnny Sharpe was nowhere in sight. Longtree and Cort were off scouting the area for signs of Johnny Sharpe.

"Maybe that stranger will leave now that his rig is fixed," Weston said.

"Yeah," Landergott said, "and maybe not."

Longtree and Cort returned and they didn't look at all happy.

"You find him?" Landergott asked.

"We didn't find him, Steve, but we found a fresh-dug grave out behind the house," Cort said.

"His?" Weston asked.

"Who else's, you fool," Landergott said. "So, the stranger's taken a hand in the game. He ain't going away—not on his own, anyway."

"Shouldn't we tell the sheriff?" Weston asked.

"Sure, why not bring the law into this? We'll tell them that Johnny was raping the women—or whatever the hell the fool was doing—and the stranger caught him in the act and killed him."

"And buried him," Cort said. "That means the stranger ain't about to bring the law into this, either."

"Maybe not, but whatever he's gonna do he's gonna

be sorry he put his nose in my business."

"Maybe before we make a move on him we should find out who he is?" Marty Cort said.

"Good idea, Marty. And who better to tell us than the blacksmith? Let's get back to town and ask the big man some questions."

They all turned and walked back to where they had left their horses.

When they were mounted, Landergott said, "Longtree."

"Yeah?"

"Why don't you go and check out the man's rig and see what you can find out about him? We'll meet you back in town."

Longtree nodded, and rode off toward the rig while the others headed back to Turner's Basin.

TWENTY-ONE

Papa Teng sent the boys outside, and Soong Teng and Donna went into Soong Teng's room so Papa and Clint could talk at the table.

Papa told Clint the story of the gold robbery and explained how he had become friends with Khan.

"Khan told me where the gold was—sort of. He said it was a cave—" Papa Teng stopped himself short of telling Clint exactly what Khan had told him.

"That's all right, Papa. I don't need any special knowledge that your friend might have given you. I can do one of two things. I can help you find the gold, or I can simply watch your back while you find it yourself."

"Watch my back?"

"Make sure that Landergott and his friends don't get the drop on you. I would be acting as a sort of bodyguard."

"I would rather you protected my family."

"And leave you unprotected?"

"I can take care of myself."

"Not against four gunmen. Now maybe we're getting to the reason we'd need one more man."

"Like the blacksmith?"

"Yes. He'd be a perfect choice to protect your family."

"And what would he want in return?"

"You could hire him strictly to protect your family and tell him nothing about the gold, or you could promise him a small piece of the gold for his help."

"And when we found the gold, what if he wanted to take it for himself?"

"That's what I'm here for, remember? Besides, I consider myself a pretty good judge of character. I think if we tell this man the truth and promise him ample payment, we'd be able to trust him."

"And you?" Papa Teng said. "Can I trust you?"

With your women, no, Clint found himself thinking.

"Yes, you could. I don't want your gold, Papa. Believe me."

"Do you want to know how much there is?"

"That's not necessary."

"It is stolen, you know."

"I know that, but I don't want to know when, or from where. That's your business, too. I just want to keep your family and you safe until you find it. What you do with it afterward—whether you keep it or turn it in for the reward—that's up to you."

"Reward?"

"Well, of course wherever it was stolen from there would be a reward for its return."

Obviously, Papa Teng had not thought of that.

"How much of a reward?"

"Ten, perhaps twenty percent."

"Considerably less than I would get if I keep it."

"But honest."

"I am not a dishonest man," Papa Teng said tightly.

"I didn't say you were."

Papa Teng thought over his options and finally said, "Very well."

"Very well . . . what?"

"I will accept your offer to help."

"Specifically."

"To . . . watch my back, as you said."

"And the blacksmith?"

"If you can get him to agree, yes, I will accept him to guard my family."

"I have to go into town tomorrow to talk to him about a team of horses for my rig. I want to bring the rig back here. That's when I'll talk to him about the job, strictly a paying job."

"Tell him . . . whatever you think it is necessary to tell him."

"I'll tell him what I think he needs to know, Papa, and that's all."

Papa Teng nodded.

Clint started to get up and then Papa Teng said, "I appreciate your help, Mr. Adams."

"Clint."

Papa Teng looked at him, then nodded and without change of his usual dour, pained expression said, "Clint."

TWENTY-TWO

Longtree reached the rig before Landergott and the others reached town. He dismounted, looked around, and then entered the now upright wagon.

The inside was in a state of total disarray, and he began digging through everything, trying to find something that would tell him who the stranger was. One thing was obvious: with all the guns and equipment that were inside, the man was either a gun salesman, or a gunsmith.

Finally, he found some letters tied together with string, tore them open, and began scanning them. They were all from different people, some men, some women, some very personal—whoever this man was, he was apparently successful with women—and they all began "Dear Clint." He looked through the first pack thoroughly and couldn't find an envelope.

He found a second pack of letters, didn't bother

reading them, simply tore open the string and fanned the letters out all over the place until he found an envelope.

He picked the envelope up, read it, stared off into space, read it again, and then scrambled out of the rig and onto his horse.

He had to tell Landergott who they were dealing with.

At the moment, Landergott, Marty Cort, and Cole Weston were preparing to deal with the blacksmith, who apparently arrived back in town just minutes ahead of them.

They put their horses up in the livery, which had no connection with the blacksmith.

"How are we going to handle this?" Cort asked.

"We're just gonna ask the man a question, that's all."

Landergott entered the blacksmith's shop with Cort on one side of him and Weston on the other. Their stance, as far as Horace Stoneman was concerned, shrieked of belligerence.

"What do you fellas want? I'm busy," Stoney said, proving he could be pretty belligerent himself.

"I've got a question to ask you, blacksmith, and my advice is that you just answer it."

Stoney narrowed his eyes and said, "You want to ask questions, go talk to a bartender. They love answering questions."

"That's not the right attitude, blacksmith," Landergott said.

The two men took a few moments to size each other up, as big men will do. An unbiased observer would have said that Horace Stoneman was the bigger man, but Steve Landergott was younger and had more solid muscle. The blacksmith, however, though he did not boast Landergott's bulging muscles, did have a raw-boned power that stood out. His beginning bulge of belly betrayed his age, but he was still a formidable-looking opponent for any man.

"Now look, friend, if you've got a question ask it. I'll see if it's one that I want to answer. If I don't, then I'd advise you and your friends to be on your way."

"That's pretty big talk for a man who isn't wearing a gun," Landergott said.

"I don't need a gun for the likes of you, friend. You, on the other hand, better get more help if you're thinking of going head to head with me."

Landergott's shoulders hunched and Cort knew that the main question was about to get lost in a confrontation of big men. He'd seen it happen before.

"Look, blacksmith," he said, breaking in, "all we want to know is the name of the stranger you just did a job for. Simple as that."

"I don't know his name," Stoneman said. "Simple as that. Now get out."

"You did a job for the man and you don't know his name?"

"I get paid in cash, friend, I don't need the name of the man who's paying me. Now take your musclebound friend and get out of my place before I throw all three of you out."

Cort stepped up next to Landergott and said, "Steve, we don't need this."

Landergott's shoulder muscles relaxed, but he pointed a thick finger at the blacksmith.

"You and me, smithy, we ain't done."

"Come back any time without your friends," Stoneman invited.

Outside Landergott stopped and said, "Before we leave . . ."

"Forget him, Steve."

"Don't tell me what to do, Marty."

"Then do what you want with him, but after we finish with the Chinaman."

"Let's go over to the saloon and wait for Longtree."

As Landergott led the way to the saloon Cort decided that he'd like to see the big smithy go up against his friend. It would be very, very interesting to see who was still on their feet when it was all over.

When Longtree got to the saloon Landergott and the others were working on their second bottle. Cort could see that Landergott was stewing over the confrontation with the big blacksmith.

Longtree walked directly to the table, sat down, poured himself a drink, and downed it.

"Did you check the rig?" Landergott asked.

"I did."

Landergott took a drink of his own and then said, "Well, what the bloody hell did you find out, then? Or is it a damned secret?"

"I found out the stranger's name."

"So? You keeping us in suspense for some reason?"

Longtree took another drink before answering.

"I found some letters—"

"Just tell us his goddamned name!"

"Clint Adams."

The man's name dropped to the table like a stick of dynamite lying in their midst.

"Adams?" Cort asked.

"As in 'Gunsmith'?" Cole Weston asked. "That Clint Adams?"

Landergott sat forward and said, "How many Clint Adams do you think there are, stupid?"

"Hey, Landergott," Weston said, "I signed on to take some gold away from an old Chinaman and his family. You didn't say nothing about going up against the Gunsmith."

"So we go up against the Gunsmith, so what?" Landergott said. "Take away his gun and he's just another man."

"Yeah," Weston said pointedly, "but who's gonna take away his gun?"

"Don't worry," Landergott said. "I'll figure something out."

Marty Cort stayed quiet through the whole thing, working steadily on the whiskey. He fancied himself a decent gun—an *excellent* hand with a gun if he'd been drinking—and wasn't particularly frightened of the Gunsmith, or any other gunman. Respectful yes, but not frightened.

At least learning the stranger's name had accomplished one thing. From the look on Landergott's face, he was concentrating on the Gunsmith now, and had forgotten about the blacksmith.

TWENTY-THREE

Clint was not surprised, and more than a little grateful, to find that his offer to sleep in the main room with the boys was accepted. It saved him the possible awkward problem of having Donna visit him in the night again. Now that she was back in her own room, in her own bed, he could rest easy.

Or so he thought.

He slept across the room from where the boys were sleeping, in the place Donna had slept—without the blanketed privacy that she had enjoyed, of course.

During the night his always alert ear picked up the sound of someone entering the room, and then he felt a hand on his shoulder.

"Clint—"

"Shhh."

It was Donna.

"Come into my room."

"No, Donna—"

"Come into my room or I will scream."

Annoyed, he threw back his blanket quietly and followed her to her room. As he entered and closed the door behind her, she pulled her nightgown up over her head and discarded it. In the soft glow of the storm lamp she was beautiful, all shadows and curves and soft skin.

"Donna, you can't keep threatening me like this."

"Why not?" she asked, moving closer to him. He could feel the heat from her body. Her hand touched his crotch, where a telltale bulge pushed against his pants.

"Don't tell me you don't like it?"

"Anywhere else but here, under your father's roof."

"This is not my father's roof," she said, sounding angry suddenly. "This is not my home! I do not know where my home is anymore. Clint, I want you to take me with you when you leave here."

"What?"

"Are you leaving soon?"

"No."

"Why not?"

"I've decided to stay and help your father."

"Help him search for that gold?"

"Yes."

"But that's wonderful!" she said. She threw her arms around his neck and pressed her naked body tightly against him. Her breasts crushed themselves against his chest, and her crotch pressed solidly against his.

"With your share we can leave together and go to San Francisco."

"My share?"

"Yes," she said, her lips pressed against his neck.

"You are getting a share, aren't you?"

"No."

He felt her body stiffen.

"What do you mean, no?" she asked, drawing back so she could look into his face.

"I'm helping your father—and you, I thought—to pay you all back for helping me."

"But that's crazy," she said. "You must take a share of the gold—if not for yourself, then for me. Give it to me, so I can leave."

"You want to leave your family?"

"Yes," she hissed, "oh, yes. I want to go somewhere and live, Clint, really live—and I want you to go with me."

"I can't, Donna."

"Would you rather go with my mother?"

He didn't answer.

"Are you going to tell me that you haven't made love to my mother, right here under my father's roof?" she demanded with a sneer.

"Donna, you don't understand—"

"I understand that my mother is beautiful, and my father is old." She took his hands in hers and put them on her breasts. He itched to squeeze them, but resisted. "I understand, Clint, really I do, but my mother will never leave my father."

"I don't want her to."

"You don't love her?"

"Of course not."

"And do you love me?"

"No."

"But you could, if you let yourself."

"Donna—"

"Clint, with gold and with me, it could be so good

for you. I could make it very good for you."

Her hands went to his belt and started to undo his pants, but he grabbed her hands and stopped her.

"I will scream," she said.

"Yes," he said, suddenly angry, "you will, but not for the reasons you think."

He pushed her away from him so that she fell onto the bed. He discarded his pants and advanced on her, his erection an angry red and throbbing.

He pinned her hands over her head, which lifted her breasts. He sucked her nipples and breasts until she was moaning and writhing beneath him and then suddenly, savagely, he entered her, thrusting so hard that she caught her breath.

Still holding her arms over her head he began to drive into her, pausing each time he was fully inside her and moving his hips, and then withdrawing and driving again. Soon, she was gasping, fighting to keep her hips in unison with his thrusts, but he was moving erratically, so that she couldn't find his tempo. It was maddening for her and she began to sob, at the same time trying to keep quiet.

Suddenly, she knew what he meant when he said that she would not scream for her own reasons.

He was making love to her brutally, in such a way that she could not match his tempo, not find her own pleasure. Oh, she was experiencing pleasure, all right, but he was controlling just how much, and if she didn't scream from frustration she would scream when her pent-up orgasm finally did come, releasing her.

Or so he thought.

Fiercely, she fought him, moving her hips with him. She swore she would not scream for him, and that his pleasure would be as intense as hers when it came.

Soon the bed became something of a battlefield, and they were both straining to continue their contest in silence, without waking the rest of the house.

As he had realized the night before, she was definitely not a virgin, and although she was still naive in some ways—all that talk about love—not as innocent as she strove to appear in the company of her parents.

Finally, he decided to end it. He allowed her to find his rhythm, and they moved together after that until they both came together. She pushed her face against his chest, smothering her cries, and he groaned into the sheet next to her head and released her hands. Immediately she reached for him, clutching him close to her while they rode the waves of pleasure they were both feeling . . .

He stood up then, pulling his pants on. She remained on the bed spent and breathless, unable to rise.

"You're a little vixen, Donna," he said. "I don't think either of your parents know you very well."

"Neither . . . do you . . ." she said breathlessly.

"No, and I don't think I want to. Don't try threatening me again. I don't think your parents would be as surprised as you think by anything you did."

"They still see me as a child," she said, staring at him boldly. "I am a woman, Clint."

"You don't have to tell me that, Donna. I know that probably better than anyone."

"I won't have to threaten you into coming to me," she said, pushing herself up to her elbows. Her forehead was damp, and her dark hair was matted to it. It was cold, yet a rivulet of perspiration wended its way between her breasts and down to her navel. He followed its progress with a fascination he wished he didn't feel. Under other circumstances he would have liked nothing better than to lick the sweat from between her breasts. This one—Donna, Sooni, whatever she wanted to be called—had suddenly become a dangerous woman, because she was young and beautiful, and knew how to use those things to her advantage—and she certainly hadn't learned that under her father's roof.

She was breathing hard, her nostrils flaring, and she was lovelier than he'd ever seen her before.

"You'll come when I call, Clint Adams," she said with certainty.

"Don't you believe it," he said, moving to the door. "You're not in my league, Donna. You're just a baby."

"I'll show you what a baby I am," she said, putting one hand between her legs and opening herself up to him. "I'll show you," she said, and laughed softly.

He went into the main room, to his little patch of floor, and lay down, not a little breathless himself.

She was something else, little Sooni, but he had yet to figure out what.

He would, though.

He would.

TWENTY-FOUR

In the morning he rose early, saddled Duke, and left for town. Papa Teng would know where he went. Let Donna worry that maybe he had left without her.

When he got to town he headed straight for the blacksmith's shop. He realized that he probably could have purchased a team from the livery, but he wanted to cement his relationship with the blacksmith, Stoney.

After all, it had started out so well.

Landergott had also risen early. He had too much on his mind to sleep. Besides, Marty Cort's snoring got louder the more he drank the night before. Landergott was looking out the window when Clint Adams rode into town.

So that was the Gunsmith, huh? And he headed straight for the blacksmith's shop. What other business did the two of them have together?

He settled down to see how long Adams would be
with the blacksmith. If his enemies were joining
forces, maybe he'd be able to kill them all at the same
time.

"You again? So soon?" the blacksmith said to Clint
as he walked in.

"We have to talk about a team."

Stoneman wiped his hands on a rag and approached
Clint.

"You can get one at the livery cheaper than you can
from me."

"Is their stock as good as yours?"

"Mine is shit," he said, "but theirs is worse. What
do you need?"

"Just two horses to get me out of here—when I go,
that is."

"You mean you're not leaving here as soon as you
can?"

"No."

The blacksmith snorted in disgust. "Why the hell
not?"

"What's wrong with the place?"

"Listen, friend—"

"Adams, Clint Adams."

"If I could get a grubstake together I'd be out of
here like—what did you say?"

"When?"

"Just now."

"About what?"

"Your name, damn it. What did you say your name
was?"

"Clint Adams."

Stoneman looked down at the ground, rubbing his

jaw with a big, sausage-fingered hand.

"I know that name."

"Maybe you do—"

"No, I really do."

"I'm interested in that team, and I think I might be able to help you with that grubstake you were talking about."

"Is that a fact?"

"Is there somewhere we can talk?"

"You want a drink?"

"Isn't it a little early for the saloon to be open?"

"I'm not talking about the saloon. Come on."

Clint followed Stoney to the back of his shop into a small office where the man produced a bottle of whiskey. It was early for Clint to start drinking, but he accepted the proffered bottle and took a swig.

"Now, tell me about this grubstake."

Clint told Stoneman a story. It was about a Chinaman who had something of value tucked away, who told another Chinaman about it. Then the first Chinaman got killed, and now the second one was in danger of meeting the same fate.

"Before he can find this something of value?"

"Right."

"And what is this something?"

"Well . . . I can tell I can trust you, Stoney—"

"A statement like that makes me wonder if I can trust you. Why don't you just tell it to me straight, Adams, without the song and dance?"

"You don't belong here, you know that?"

"That's about all I know. What about it?"

"It's a cache of gold."

"There isn't any gold in these hills—"

"There is, but only because somebody put it there."

"Who?"

"The man who stole it."

"Stole it from who, and when?"

"I didn't ask that. It doesn't have any bearing on what we're talking about."

"And just what *are* we talking about, here? It's starting to get a little muddled."

"We're talking about grubstake for you."

"And what do I have to do for this grubstake?"

"Just keep some people alive."

"Like who?"

"A couple of women, maybe a couple of young boys."

"While you do what?"

"Keep the old man alive so he can find his gold."

"What's to keep me from taking the gold for myself?"

"I told you, Stoney, I trust you."

"But can I trust you?"

"I'm telling you the truth, aren't I?"

"I got it," Stoney said abruptly, completely out of context with the way the conversation was going.

"Got what?"

"Your name," Stoney said. "I know who you are. You're the fella they call the Gunsmith."

"Guilty," Clint said with a sour look. He tried to wash it away with a swig of whiskey.

"And you're hiring on to protect this Chinaman and his family?"

"I'm not being hired, Stoney, I'm offering them my services."

"For free?" Stoney looked dubious.

"I owe them."

"*I* don't."

"And *you'll* get paid."

"How much?"

"Well . . . that depends."

"Is it open to discussion?"

"Sure."

"Between you, me, and the Chinaman?"

"Right."

"So what are we waiting for. Let's go," Stoney said, standing up.

"This won't be your usual kind of work, you know."

"Look, I think I already met your opposition."

"What do you mean?"

"I should talk, but a big, ugly-looking fella and two friends of his were in here asking about you."

"What did they want?"

"They wanted your name. I didn't have it then, and I wouldn't have given it to them if I did."

"Why not?"

"Because I didn't like them, especially that big fella. Flexing his muscles like I should melt when he did. Him and me are going to go at it sooner or later, I might as well be getting paid for it when we do."

"All right," Clint said, standing up. "Hey, wait a minute."

"What now?"

"What about my team?"

"Shit," Stoney said, "if what you say is true, and we can negotiate an equitable price, you can have the goddamned team. I'll throw it in."

"Well, let me look them over while I'm here, then."

"They're in the back. Let's go."

TWENTY-FIVE

"What's so interesting out the window?"

Landergott turned and looked at Cort, who was a sight sitting up with his feet on the floor. All he was wearing was his long underwear.

"Adams is in town."

"Oh, yeah? Maybe we should—"

"Maybe you should just keep quiet and let me do the thinking, Marty. I think your brain is still in a fog from drinking."

"Hey, Steve—"

"Shut up," Landergott said, looking out the window again. "He's been with the blacksmith a long time."

"Settling up his bill?"

"Maybe—and maybe he's figuring on getting a little help."

"You mean we got to face the Chinaman, Adams, and the big blacksmith?"

"If we get them all in one place we can take care

of them all at the same time."

"And maybe we need a little more help."

"And how would you suggest we get it? There ain't a telegraph office in this town. Besides, you looking to share the gold with somebody else?"

"I was just thinking—"

"Forget thinking, Marty. I told you that. You ain't fit for it. Let's just see when Adams comes out of the blacksmith shop—and what with."

A half an hour later Clint Adams and the blacksmith came out. Clint was leading two sorry-looking horses, unsaddled, and the blacksmith one saddled mount. By this time Cort had dressed and was standing next to Landergott.

"So he bought some horses," Cort said, turning away from the window.

"You see Adams's horse, don't you?"

"Sure. Big black gelding."

"Why would he need another saddle horse. He needs a team for his rig, but why a saddle horse?"

"Then why'd he buy one?"

"He didn't. Watch."

As they watched, the blacksmith mounted the other saddle horse and then he and Clint Adams rode out of town, Adams still leading the team.

"Why's the blacksmith going with him?" Cort asked.

"Because he's thrown in with him, why else?"

"What do we do now?"

"You might be right about us needing more help," Landergott said. "See what kind of talent this town has to offer. Sooner or later they have to split up. Adams will have to go with the old Chinaman looking for the gold. That leaves the blacksmith to look after the women. We have our friend Johnny to thank for that. He never could keep it in his pants."

"What do I offer the local boys?"

Landergott shrugged. "See what their idea of big money is and give it to them. We can afford it."

"Right."

"Meet me in the saloon—and try to stay sober until I get there."

TWENTY-SIX

Clint and Stoney went to the rig and hitched up the new team.

"I hope they get me where I want to go," Clint said. "In fact, I hope they get us back to the house."

"They'll do as a temporary team," Stoney assured him. "Just don't push them too hard, or expect too much of them."

"Don't worry about that."

Clint went into the back of the rig to look things over and knew immediately that someone had been there. His letters were strewn all about, and they had been tied tightly with heavy twine. Not even the accident would have tossed them around that way—and, besides, he'd already been into the wagon once, and they hadn't been tossed around then.

No, someone had been there snooping, and the only thing they could have been looking for was his name.

"Well, I guess they got what they came to you for,"

he said when he stepped outside.

"What do you mean?"

Clint told him.

"Then they know who you are. Maybe they'll pull back now, move on."

"Not hardly. I don't flatter myself as much as that—especially not when there's gold involved."

"Then we might as well get back to the house and get this job underway."

On the way to the house, Stoney asked, "If they know they're dealing with you, wouldn't it follow that they'd try to get some other help?"

"Possibly—especially if they knew they were dealing with you, as well. Anybody in town want a piece of you?"

"They'd have to stand in line, but I'll tell you, I think that big fella—what's his name?"

"Landergott."

"Yeah, Landergott. I think he'd like to save me for himself."

"Then they'd get some fellas who had guns and weren't afraid to use them, and they'd get somebody they could buy cheap."

"Shit," Stoney said, "you could buy the whole town of Turner's Basin cheap."

"That's what I was afraid of."

When they got to the house they drove the rig around back and unhitched the horses. There wasn't room in the small shack for the horses, and Clint didn't want to crowd Duke anyway. They left them picketed outside, and went into the house.

When the boys saw Stoney they looked up at him in awe, as they had the first time they saw him. He was the biggest man they had ever seen.

"Mr. Adams tells me you need help," Stoney said to Papa Teng.

"Yes."

"And that my price should be made with you."

"That is correct."

They eyed each other for a few moments and then Stoney said, "Well, you pay me what you think is fair—what you think your family's lives are worth. All I'm looking for is enough money to get out of this place and to somewhere civilized."

Clint left the two men together, because he felt that they would probably dicker a while longer. He went outside and began to walk in a circle around the house, widening it as he went. Finally, he found what he wanted. A place where a man or men had obviously spent some time sitting. There were spent cigarettes and cigarillos lying around which had probably been smoked in cupped hands to hide the glow from the house. As he had surmised earlier, they had been watched—probably even before he arrived, certainly since.

He went back in the house and found Stoney smiling and joking with the boys. Papa Teng looked his dour self, but a price had apparently been set.

"Is it done?" he asked.

Papa Teng looked at him and Stoney said, "It's done. This little man drives a hard bargain."

"But a fair one?"

"It's fair. His family is in good hands."

"You'll need a gun."

Stoney frowned and said, "I don't like them, but no doubt you're right."

"We can get one from my rig. You'll also have to settle your affairs in town."

"What affairs? I'll close the shop and leave it for

whoever wants it. There isn't much I want to take with me from there. I can go in and be back tonight, just after dark."

"All right, but be careful. I don't want to lose you before we even get started."

"I can get into town and out without anyone being the wiser."

"Let's go out and get you that gun."

Outside at the rig Clint said, "You'll need something that won't fall apart in your big hands."

As Clint climbed into the back of the rig Stoney stuck his head in and said, "That's a tight-fisted little bugger in there, even with his family's lives on the line."

"But did you get a fair price?"

"Who's to say what's fair. I got what I need to get going."

"Here's a gun you can handle," Clint said. "A Walker Colt. It's big and it's sturdy."

"That's fine."

"Take it with you. When you get back I can clean it up for you."

"All right, as long as it will fire."

"Oh, it'll fire," Clint said, handing it to the blacksmith. In the man's big hand the gun suddenly shrunk. Clint found himself hoping that it was extremely sturdy.

He walked Stoney to his horse and the big man mounted.

"You should let me ride your horse," the blacksmith said. "He's more my size."

"You wouldn't be able to stay on him."

"No," Stoney said, eyeing Duke appreciatively, "I don't believe I would."

TWENTY-SEVEN

In town Marty Cort was able to round up three men with guns who'd fire them for a cheap price. He brought them to the saloon to await Landergott's arrival. When he arrived, he had Longtree and Weston in tow.

"These the men you found?"

"They're all the town had to offer," Cort said.

"Whatsa matter with us?" one of them asked.

"For one thing, you talk too much," Landergott said, walking up to the three men. They were all of a kind, young, dirty, hungry. Landergott had no doubt that they'd kill each other for two bits. "You fellas better know that I'm in charge. You do what I say without question."

"What if we—"

Landergott backhanded the speaker viciously, knocking him down and splitting his lip. The man went for his gun, but Landergott reached down and took hold of his hand, holding it in his own massive paw. He squeezed until tears came to the man's eyes.

"Like I said, no questions. Right?"

"R-right."

Landergott let the man's hand go and backed away. Cort was ready just in case the man went for his gun.

"I didn't break your hand because I might need you, friend."

The man flexed his fingers to make sure they still worked right.

"Either of you got any questions?"

"No," the other two men said together.

"Did Cort make arrangements for your pay?"

"Yes," one of them said.

"All right, then. All you have to do is be ready when I call on you. Now get out."

The two picked up the one from the floor and the three of them left the saloon.

Cort took his hand off his gun and said, "You sure know how to make friends, Landergott."

"I'm not out to make friends, Cort. I'm out to get what I'm after."

"What's our next move, then?"

"By now Adams knows that we've been watching the house."

"So we don't watch anymore?"

"No, we do watch, just not from the same vantage point, and not as close. We can draw back and wait for him and the old man to go searching."

"And then what? We follow them?" Cort asked.

"No, I think it may be time for us to make a positive move."

"Like what?"

"Like grabbing his family."

"How do we do that?"

"We don't," Landergott said, looking at the saloon door, "they do."

"You're going to send them after the women?"

"That's right. For one thing, it will tell us how much trouble that blacksmith is gonna be."

"If he really is throwing in with them."

"We'll know that tonight."

"How?"

"If he's going with them he'll pull out. If he does, then we'll send those three in tomorrow. Once we have the Chinaman's family, he'll tell us what we want to know."

"We should have gone this way from the beginning," Cort said.

"Maybe," Landergott said, surprising Cort. It was almost an admittance that he was wrong. "We'll find out tomorrow."

TWENTY-EIGHT

Just before dinner Clint went outside the house to look around. A few moments later, Soong Teng came out.

"Dinner will be ready in five minutes."

"I'll be in."

She didn't go back in, though.

"Is something wrong?"

"That big man. He will be staying with us?"

"With you and the boys, yes."

"Beginning tomorrow?"

"Yes."

"And you?"

"I'll go with Papa Teng to look for the gold."

"The boys, they will be disappointed."

"No they won't. I'll explain that they're needed here to protect you and Sooni."

"That will help."

"Ling is sixteen, Soong Teng, old enough to handle

a gun. With your permission—"

"A gun?"

"It may come to that."

"I can shoot."

"I'll get you a gun, as well."

"Donna—Sooni, she is not a child anymore."

How well I know that, Clint thought.

"I'll give you an extra gun just in case, but I don't think it will be necessary. Stoney should be able to handle anything that comes along."

"Yes, he is very large."

"And strong."

"Yes."

The conversation seemed over, but still she did not return inside.

"Soong Teng?"

"I wish Papa had never heard about the gold," she said fervently.

"Maybe, if you talked with him—"

"I have spoken with him, but he does not listen. He wants the gold for his family, he says."

"I believe him."

"In the beginning, perhaps. Now I think he wants the gold just to have it. He is obsessed."

"That is what happens with men and gold."

"It is terrible."

"Yes, it is."

She hugged her arms, as if she'd just realized that it was cold out, and said, "I will put dinner on the table."

"I'll be in."

After she went back inside Clint walked around a bit. He didn't think Landergott and his friends would return to the same place to watch, but he knew they were watching—from further off, perhaps, but watching nevertheless.

Maybe he should be playing this differently. Maybe he should go to town and face Landergott and the others. That would be looking for a confrontation, though, and someone was sure to die. He wanted to avoid that if it was at all possible.

With good reason, though, he didn't think it would be, but he had to make the effort.

He went inside to have dinner.

After dinner Clint went outside to wait for Stoney. He wasn't there ten minutes when he heard a horse approaching. He didn't see the big blacksmith until he had almost reached the house.

"Let's put your horse in the back," Clint said, walking Stoney back there.

While Stoney was unsaddling his horse Clint said, "Let's find some stuff we can make torches out of."

"Torches?"

"Yeah. Even with your size I wasn't sure it was you until you were almost on top of me. I want to light this area up like daylight, or pretty damn near."

"All right."

"We'll take four-hour watches, you and me."

"Fine."

"I'm going to give the wife, Soong Teng, a gun. She says she knows how to use it."

"Whatever you say, but I don't think I'll need the help."

"Also the oldest son."

"If you think it's necessary."

"I'm leaving the boys behind with you, and I want them to think they're helping. Also he's sixteen. That's old enough to learn how to use a gun."

Stoney took a canvas sack that looked more empty than full off his saddle.

"That your stuff?"

"I'll be traveling light."

"Best way, I guess."

"How about you and this rig?"

"What about it?"

"Your rep says—"

"I fix guns, Stoney. To do that I need my tools."

"You mean, you really are a gunsmith?"

"That's right. Sometimes I need to make some extra money."

"I thought you'd . . ."

"I'd what?"

"You know . . . hire out . . ."

"I don't hire out my gun. Don't believe every rep you hear."

"I guess not. Sorry."

"That's all right. Let's get those torches set up."

They went inside and between old clothes in the house, some storm-lamp oil, and tree limbs, they were able to set up some torches in front of the house.

"What about the back?" Stoney asked.

"They won't be able to come around back without alerting the horses, and they'll alert us."

"Yours, maybe. My nag'll be dead asleep."

"It was mine I was thinking of."

When the torches were set and it was almost time to turn in Clint took Ling outside with him.

"I will be going with your father tomorrow, Ling."

"Yes, with us."

"No, you and your brother will be staying here."

"Here? Why?"

"Mr. Stoneman is going to need your help protecting your mother and sister."

"What about Chang?"

"He will have to stay, also. You will have to help make him understand."

The boy wanted to argue, but Clint could see him mulling it over, and finally he accepted it. It made him feel like a man to be asked to protect his mother and his sister.

"All right, Clint."

"Take a walk with me."

They walked around back to Clint's rig. He went inside and came out with a small .32 caliber pistol.

Without loading it he drilled Ling in the proper usage of it. The boy was a quick study, and the gun fit his hand. In a year or less, however, he'd need a larger one.

When Clint was convinced that the boy knew how to use the gun, he loaded it.

"Now you must understand, you are only to use this if your safety, or the safety of your family depends on it. First, you must depend on Mr. Stoneman — Stoney — but if something goes wrong, you use this gun. Do you understand?"

"I understand, Clint," the boy said sincerely. "You can depend on me."

"I know I can, Ling, or I wouldn't be giving you the gun."

They started back to the house, but Clint had one other thing to tell Ling.

"Don't show this gun to your brother, all right?"

"I understand. I am the older, I should not argue with him. I will not show him the gun."

"Good . . . man," Clint said, catching himself before

he could say "Good boy."

Ling appreciated that.

Still later Clint gave Soong Teng the Colt New Line.

"Do you need me to show you how to use it?"

"No," she said, "I know how to use it."

"All right. I gave Ling a gun also, and he knows how and when to use it. He also knows when not to use it. Do you understand?"

"Yes," she said, "I understand. I must go to bed now."

She went inside, and Stoney came out.

"Everybody armed and ready?" he asked.

"Yes," Clint said, hoping he had done the right thing. "Armed and ready. You take the first watch, Stoney."

TWENTY-NINE

Landergott, Cort, Weston, and Longtree went to the blacksmith's barn that night.

"Closed up tight," Longtree said.

"Let's break in," Landergott said. "I want to make sure he's gone."

They went around the side and broke a window. Longtree climbed in and then opened one of the doors for the others to enter.

They looked around, but from what they could see it looked like the blacksmith had left for good.

"His desk drawers are all open," Longtree said, "like he took what he wanted and left the rest."

"That settles it, then. He's taken up with the China-man and Adams," Landergott said.

"I don't know, Landergott," Longtree said. "The Gunsmith and that blacksmith throwing in with the Chinaman." It was clear that the situation as it now stood was not to Longtree's liking.

"We still outnumber them."

"Don't tell me you're scared, Longtree," Marty Cort sneered. He was more than a little drunk.

"If you weren't drunk I'd kill you for that, Cort. I ain't scared of nobody—but I am a careful man." He looked at Landergott. "Instead of taking them altogether maybe we ought to pick them off one at a time."

"You calling the shots now, Longtree?"

"I'm making a suggestion."

"I'll think about it," Landergott said. "Let's go back to the hotel and wait for Weston to get back. I want to hear what he has to say."

"Where'd he go?" Longtree asked.

"Up to take a look."

Longtree and Cort looked at each other. They never would have guessed that they were both thinking the same thing. Landergott just didn't seem at all sure how he wanted to play it, and they were starting to wonder if they'd ever see any of that gold at all.

"What the hell are you waiting for?" Landergott asked. "Let's go."

When they got back to the hotel they didn't have long to wait before Weston returned.

"They got that place all lit up with torches. We wouldn't be able to get near it."

"They post watches?" Landergott asked.

"Yep. The blacksmith is taking the first watch, sitting out there calm as you please. I could have picked him off with one rifle shot."

"Everybody seems to want to make their own decisions now," Landergott said, shaking his head. "Why don't we split up and see who gets to the gold first?"

The other three men looked at each other.

"We ain't saying that, Landergott," Weston said.

"Then you and Longtree get out and go to your own room. In the morning I'll talk to those other three and we'll send them on ahead."

They left and Marty Cort reclined on his bed, taking a bottle of whiskey from underneath his pillow.

Landergott gave Cort a sour look and sat on his own bed. Tomorrow, he'd find out just how much trouble the blacksmith was going to be.

After that, he'd turn his attention to the Gunsmith.

THIRTY

Clint and Papa Teng left the next morning to look for the gold. Papa Teng said there were a series of caves on a particular slope that might yield the gold. They exited one above the other, which was the series that Khan had told him about. He did not seem to realize that he had given his great secret away, but Clint didn't think anything of it. There were a lot of mountain slopes that had caves in them, and more than a few had caverns above caverns.

Clint took Duke with him, but Papa Teng insisted that he would rather walk. Clint did not argue with the old Chinese for fear of offending him.

Above the house, on a ridge, Landergott watched as Clint and Papa Teng left. With him were Cort, Weston, and Longtree, and the three young toughs from town.

"You fellas know who that is?" Landergott asked.

They looked down and saw the blacksmith, Stoney, standing in front of the house.

"Sure, that's the high and mighty blacksmith," one of them said.

"Thinks he's better'n everybody else in Turner's Basin," another said.

This would work out fine, Landergott decided. The three of them seemed to have a healthy dislike of the blacksmith.

"Well, that's your target."

"Hell, we can pick him off—"

"No, I want you to go down there and kill him, but not with your guns. You got knives?"

"Sure."

"Use them."

The three young men exchanged glances.

"Come on," Landergott said, "you're getting paid. Get moving."

When they didn't move he said, "You're not afraid of him, are you?"

"Hell, 'course not!" one of them said.

"Then move! And remember, if he takes a bullet from one of you, the three of you don't get paid."

The three men started their descent from the ridge, and Longtree came up next to Landergott.

"What's the idea of making them face him close up?"

"While he's fighting with them, we're gonna slip right in there and take what we want."

"Which is?"

"The women."

"What for?"

"We're gonna trade that old Chinaman his women for his gold."

"You think he's found it?"

"Maybe not, but he knows what landmark to look for. With that information we can probably find it ourselves."

"He's been looking for a long time," Cort reminded Landergott.

"Yeah, but he's just one man. The four of us will be able to find it easy once we know what he knows."

"And after he tells us, are we gonna just give the women back to him?"

Landergott looked at Cort and said, "Sure, Marty— after we're done with them."

Stoney saw the three men approaching the house and recognized them immediately as Turner's Basin's filth. What were they doing out here?

"Hey, blacksmith," one of them called.

"What do you want?"

"Whatcha doing way out here?"

"None of your business. Don't come any closer, either."

"What's wrong with you, blacksmith? We're just looking for a little water, you know? We're thirsty."

"Keep walking toward town, you'll be there in a couple of hours."

"We're thirsty now," one of them said, and all three kept moving forward, fanning out. Right away Stoney knew he'd made a mistake. If they rushed him he'd only be able to shoot one of them before the other two got him, and if they simply drew on him, he didn't even know if he'd be able to get one. He wasn't that good a shot.

"Come on, blacksmith. Be sociable."

From behind him Stoney heard the door open and heard Ling say, "What's wrong, Mr. Stoney?"

"Back inside, Ling. Look to your family."

"But—"

"Get!"

Ling moved back inside and slammed the door.

The three men kept moving closer to him, showing no signs of going for their guns.

"How come you're so high and mighty, blacksmith? Huh? How come you think you're better than us?"

"A mangy dog is better than any of you."

One of them produced a knife now, and the other two followed. They were spread out with a good ten feet between them. Too late Stoney decided to use the Walker Colt.

He pulled it from his belt and one of them yelled, "Look out. He's got a gun."

They rushed him, and in his haste to fire Stoney missed clean. Before he could fire again the three of them were on him. One of them lunged at him with the knife and it deflected off the gun, knocking it from his grasp. Another slashed at him and opened a wound on his shoulder. He stretched out his hand and grabbed the third man by the throat with one hand and used the other to break his arm over his knee. He swung the wounded man into the other two, knocking them off balance.

Stoney moved away from the house now so that he'd have room behind him. The injured man was lying on the ground, clutching his broken arm. The other two advanced on Stoney, waving their knives in front of them.

"Why don't you use your guns?" he asked, curiosity getting the better of him.

"If we use the guns we don't get paid."

So that was it. They'd been hired to kill him, but why with knives? The only reason he could think of was that it would be a diversion—or maybe Landergott wanted to kill him himself. He was welcome to try, once he disposed of these three.

"Come on, then," Stoney said. "Let's see what you can do."

They rushed him, and he moved forward to meet them instead of simply standing his ground and defending himself. His strategy surprised them, and as they slashed at him, one of them missed while one opened a cut on his right side. By then, however, he had hold of each of them by a shoulder, and he exerted all the pressure he could.

Both men were driven to their knees by the pain, and one of them dropped his knife. The other was holding the knife in his left hand while Stoney was squeezing his right shoulder, and he swung the blade now and buried it in Stoney's huge thigh.

The blacksmith let out a bellow of pain. He released the shoulder of the man who had stabbed him and struck him on the side of the neck with a fist like a ham. The man hit the ground and didn't move.

Turning his attention to the other man he released his shoulder, grabbed him by the throat, and lifted him up off the ground with both hands. Too late he saw that the man had decided to use his gun. He drew it and would have shot Stoney in the belly except for the fact that a shot rang out and Stoney could feel the man's body jerk in his hands. He dropped the dead body to the ground and turned to see who had helped him.

It was Landergott.

"You don't get off that easy, blacksmith," Landergott said. He was flanked by his three men. "Not that easy, at all. Cole."

"Yeah!"

"Go inside and bring out the rest of them."

"Right."

Cole Weston went to the door, opened it, stepped through, and staggered back out as a shot rang out. He turned to face Landergott with blood covering the side of his shirt.

"Jesus," Landergott said. "Longtree, Marty!"

Longtree and Cort approached the house cautiously. Cole was down on one knee, trying to stem the tide of blood that was gushing from his side. Cort peeked in the door and jerked back as there was another shot.

"One of them boys has got a gun!" he shouted to Landergott.

"Well, go in there and get it," Landergott said. "They're just kids and women."

Cort looked at Longtree, who drew his gun and nodded. Cort drew his gun and then both men went in low, Cort darting to the left as he entered, and Longtree to his right. There was an exchange of shots and Landergott waited to see what the outcome was.

Suddenly, a slim form came flying out and sprawled in the dirt. Landergott saw that it was a Chinese boy of about sixteen, and he was bleeding from a shoulder wound.

"Ling!" Stoney shouted.

"Stand fast, blacksmith," Landergott said, cocking the hammer on his gun.

Quickly, another Chinese boy and the two women were pushed out and followed by Longtree and Cort, who was holding a hand to his bleeding ear.

"That whelp like to shot my ear off!" he shouted. He walked over to the fallen boy and pointed his gun at him.

"Don't kill him!" Landergott said.

"Steve—"

"I said don't, Cort."

"Ah, shit!" Cort said. He backed off, then launched a kick that struck Ling in the head and flipped him over onto his back where he lay still.

The older woman, the boy's mother, gasped and ran to her fallen son, but Longtree grabbed her by the arm before she reached him. Cort turned and walked to the young one.

"Which one's yours, Steve?" Cort asked.

"Landergott! I'm bleeding!" Cole Weston complained.

"You ain't hit bad," Landergott said. He recalled that he had given one of the women to the men, and now had to make a quick decision. He was more concerned with that than with Cole Weston's wound.

"The young one," he finally said.

"Fair enough," Longtree said. He took hold of the older woman's shirt and tore it straight down. The buttons flew off and her breasts bobbed free. At the sight of them Landergott wondered if he had made the wrong choice.

"Mother!" the other boy shouted, and launched himself at Longtree, who simply backhanded him, knocking him down. The younger woman went to his aid, kneeling by him.

"Big men," Stoney said. "Striking women and children."

"You talk big, blacksmith."

"Try me, why don't you?"

"You don't look too good, blacksmith. You're bleed-ing in more than one place."

"I'm bleeding too, damn it!" Weston shouted. He'd wadded up his shirt and pressed it against his side, but even as he complained he knew he wasn't hurt badly. The bullet had gone right through.

"I'm more than fit to take care of you," Stoney said to Landergott, challenging him.

"You think so, huh?"

"I know so."

Landergott walked up to Stoney and said, "Let's see."

He shifted his gun to his left hand, then put his right hand out over his head, as if reaching to pull an apple from a tree. Stoney knew what he wanted. A test of strength. He reached up similarly, extended his hand, and joined hands with Landergott, fingers intertwined.

When Landergott felt the pressure that the blacksmith was exerting he knew right away that he couldn't match the man's strength. It was a shock to him, and he became angry. He put the barrel of the gun right up against Stoney's belly and pulled the trigger twice.

Stoney stiffened at each impact and Landergott re-leased his hand and pushed the blacksmith away from him. Stoney remained on his feet, but his hands were clutching his belly, trying to keep from bleeding to death.

"Steve!" Marty Cort shouted.

Landergott turned and fired out of reflex. He didn't know where the older woman had gotten the gun, but she was about to fire at him. His shot struck her right between the breasts, and she fell to the ground in a crumpled heap.

"Coward!" Stoney said, starting toward Landergott, extending his huge, blood-soaked hands.

"Shut up!" Landergott said, and shot the blacksmith in the head.

The big man fell to the ground on his back and it was very quiet, except for the sobbing of the younger woman. Landergott looked at her, then at the dead older woman, and knew he'd made the right choice.

"All right," he said, "let's take the girl and go." He walked to the younger boy, who was sitting on the ground, bleeding from the mouth, and said, "You understand English, boy?"

Chang's eyes were round with shock, but he managed to nod in reply to the question.

"You tell your papa and the Gunsmith that I'll trade this here young one for the location of the gold. You understand?"

"Y-yes—"

Landergott put his foot against the boy's face and pushed him onto his back.

"Let's go!"

For good measure, Landergott shot all three of the town toughs in the head, just to make sure they were dead, too.

As he walked away he had a huge erection, but he was saving it for the girl.

THIRTY-ONE

Clint and Papa Teng spent most of the day in caves, some of which extended back twenty feet or so, some a hundred and twenty feet. At one point, they divided and each of them checked their own caves. Clint felt honored by the trust Papa Teng was placing in him, and felt guilty about what had happened between himself and Papa Teng's wife and daughter.

"It'll be dark in a couple of hours," Clint said. "We'd better start back."

"Yes," Papa Teng said.

On the way back Papa Teng spoke only once.

"Tomorrow we will separate."

They had started out looking together and had only separated later in the day. By saying that he wanted to split up the next morning, Papa Teng was further illustrating the trust he now felt for Clint Adams.

Adams felt honored again—but that feeling lasted only a short while, the length of time it took them to make their way back to the house.

When they saw what had been left for them in front of the house, Clint was stunned. Papa Teng walked to his wife's side and stared down at her, his face expressionless, but Clint thought that maybe he was feeling even worse than Papa Teng at that moment.

This was his fault! If he had gone into town and faced Landergott from the start, and killed him, then this wouldn't have happened.

"She is dead," Papa Teng said calmly.

Clint was standing over Stoney and didn't bother telling Papa that the blacksmith was also dead. Instead he rushed to Ling's side and examined the boy. He'd been shot in the shoulder and apparently kicked in the head judging from the swelling, but he was alive.

"Ling is alive," he said.

"As is Chang."

Clint looked over at the younger boy, who looked to be in a state of shock.

"Let's take them inside."

He picked Ling up in his arms and carried him inside, while Papa Teng walked Chang behind him. Clint didn't bother looking closely at the other bodies. They had obviously been shot in the head.

When they were inside he laid Ling on Donna's bed and tended to the boy's wounds as best he could. He didn't think he would die from the shoulder wound, but he had lost a lot of blood as well as taken a vicious boot to the side of the head. He would be unconscious for some time.

When he came out into the main room he saw Papa Teng sitting at the table, his hands folded in front of him.

"Where's Chang?"

"He is on my bed."

"Asleep?"

"I do not think so."

"Did he say anything?"

"Yes."

"What?"

"Landergott has taken Sooni. He will trade her for the location of the gold."

"You don't know the location, but he'll probably take whatever information you can give him. He and his men will be able to cover twice the ground we can. We'll have to find him and—"

"No."

"What do you mean no?"

"I will not trade the information for Sooni."

"Papa Teng. They killed your wife and nearly killed your boys. They won't hesitate to kill Sooni."

"I will not trade."

"For the love of God, why not?"

"I have my sons."

The man seemed to think that explained it all. From what Clint knew of the Chinese culture, he knew that sons were much more important than daughters, but damn it, this wasn't China!

"That's crazy."

"We will go into the mountains. They will not find us. I know the caves well, now."

"You take those boys into the mountains and they'll freeze to death."

"We cannot leave them behind."

"We? If you think I'm just going to go gold hunting after all of this, you're a crazy old man."

Papa Teng looked at Clint and Clint recoiled from what he saw in the man's eyes. He *was* a crazy old man!

"Papa, you listen to me. I'm going to go and get Sooni back from them."

"You cannot."

"Yes, I can. I have something to trade. I'll tell Landergott what I know."

"You cannot!" Papa Teng said in an entirely different tone of voice. For the first time Clint saw a change of expression on the Chinaman's face. "You cannot give away my gold!"

"If I knew where it was I'd sure as hell give it away to get your daughter back, but I'm going to try and trade what I know for her—if I can't get her back any other way."

Papa Teng stared at Clint, then said, "Oh, I see."

"You see what?"

"You feel guilt."

"Well, of course I feel guilt, man!"

"None of this is your doing," Papa Teng said. "All of this happened because I want to find the gold. I absolve you of any responsibility."

"Like hell!" Clint shouted. "*I* don't absolve me. Tomorrow I'm going to find Sooni and bring her back." He leaned over so that he could thrust his index finger into Papa Teng's face. "When I return, if you and these boys are not still here, I'll come looking for you, Chinaman, and when I find you you'll wish you had never been born."

Clint backed away from the man in disgust and said, "I'm going outside to clean up. I'll bury Stoney and Soong Teng."

"I will bury my wife," Papa Teng said, rising.

"Well, that's something," Clint said, walking out ahead of the Chinaman.

It might have been something, but it sure as hell

wasn't enough. It was a damned sight *far* from enough.

When Clint finished burying Stoney he dragged the other three dead men away from the house and left them stacked haphazardly. He didn't know who they were and he didn't care.

He found Papa Teng standing over Soong Teng's grave and kept his distance. As Papa turned away he saw the Chinaman's face.

The man didn't even show any grief!

He had to be crazy!

After Papa had gone back into the house Clint walked over to Soong Teng's grave.

"I'm sorry, Soong Teng, I truly am. I swear I'll find Sooni and bring her back alive. That I swear to you."

He was glad now that he'd had the chance to make love to her, to help her, and no longer felt an ounce of guilt about it. Obviously, even if Papa Teng had known he wouldn't have cared. The man cared only for his gold—and possibly for his sons.

Clint wasn't all too sure about that last part.

THIRTY-TWO

The next morning Clint went out on Duke to search for Donna. He went high first, spent most of the day looking for sign of them.

At one point he had dismounted and was checking the hard ground for sign when he heard Duke give a strange whinny, like a warning. At the same moment he became aware that someone—or something—was behind him.

He stood up slowly and turned his body just enough so that he could see. What he saw made him freeze.

It was a wolf, a great big, shaggy gray wolf. The animal's muzzle was wet and dripping with saliva, and its eyes were fixed on him.

Clint was standing with his right side to the wolf, which meant that if he wanted to draw his gun he'd have to turn it to make a shot. He'd have been in a better position if his left side had been facing the animal, because then he would have been able to draw and fire across his body.

There was nothing else to do, however. He was definitely wolf food, and maybe Duke, as well, although he felt that the big gelding might have a chance against the wolf. His only chance was the ability with a gun that had given him a reputation he hated. Now he only hoped he was half as good as that rep.

He saw the wolf tense and knew he had to move now. Even as he drew, though, the wolf moved, rushing toward him and launching into a jump. He only had time for one shot, and almost as he fired the animal was on him. He felt the weight of the animal slam into him and was knocked off his feet, his gun spinning out of his hand. He rolled and kept rolling, not knowing whether the wolf was moving after him or not. He came to a stop and looked around for something, anything to use against the wolf. He grabbed a fist-sized rock and turned to throw it, but saw that he didn't have to.

The wolf was down, and apparently dead. He moved slowly toward the fallen animal, prodded it with his foot, and then turned it over. There was blood on its chest. His one shot had struck home.

Luck, he thought, pure and simple.

He picked up his gun and holstered it, then looked at Duke, who had stood his ground.

"Brave horse, right, big guy?" He patted the gelding's neck and said, "You should have been miles from here by now, looking out for yourself."

Duke gave him a baleful stare, and Clint decided that the horse had had second thoughts, and agreed.

"Next time, huh?"

He moved around to mount up and that was when

he saw them. Five Indians on horseback, looking down at him. He wondered if they had watched the whole thing with the wolf. Not an expert on Indians, he was unable to identify them by tribe, but he assumed they were the Indians that Papa Teng had talked about. If they were, then they were peaceful traders. If they weren't . . .

He and one of the braves—apparently the leader—stared at each other for a few moments, and then the brave said something to the others, and they all turned and rode away.

Wolves and Indians, Clint thought, and no sign of Landergott and Donna.

He returned to the house that night, depressed. Papa Teng was there with the boys, but whether it was as a result of his threat or not, Clint didn't know.

He checked on Chang, who was up and around and, although quiet, seemed well enough. He fixed something for the boy to eat, and then went to check on Ling.

As soon as he entered the room he knew something was wrong. Despite the coolness of the room, Ling was sweating profusely. He was burning up with fever.

"How long has he been like this?" Clint demanded to Papa Teng.

"Since the afternoon."

"What have you done about it?"

"Blankets—"

Clint turned away from Papa, saw that there were at least three blankets on Ling.

"You old fool. There's still some snow on the ground outside. Take a bucket and get some. Hurry!"

When Papa Teng returned with the snow Clint had stripped Ling naked. The boy was painfully thin, his ribs showing clearly beneath his skin. Clint took the snow and started to wash Ling down with it, hoping that the cold snow would serve to bring the fever down.

Afterward he covered the boy again, and sat with him awhile.

Later he went out and got the snow himself and repeated the process.

By morning, Ling's fever had gone down some and stayed down.

Clint went out searching again and returned that night even more depressed. He checked on Ling, and his fever had apparently broken. He fed Chang and didn't worry about what Papa Teng was eating.

At the table, drinking coffee and eating around the moldy parts of a piece of cheese, he realized what a fool he had been. He had been out there searching for sign, trying to track Landergott with his meager tracking abilities, when all the while Landergott would make sure that he was someplace that Clint and Papa Teng could find him.

In town.

"Damn it! In town!" he shouted, bringing his fist down on the table.

Papa Teng was not in the room, having retired, but Chang was sleeping in a corner and Clint looked to see if he had awakened the boy. He had not.

Tomorrow morning he would go to town and try to free Donna. If he couldn't, then he was going to have to try to barter for her life with the little bits of information he had about the gold.

For her life and, very probably, his own.

THIRTY-THREE

"What's taking them so long?" Marty Cort demanded drunkenly.

Landergott looked across the table at him in disgust. When they had returned to town with the girl they had taken over the saloon and they all slept and ate there. Now, two days gone, they were getting on each other's nerves.

The only one he wasn't getting tired of was that little China gal upstairs. He'd never get tired of the way his pecker slid into her wet little box, or the way she tasted when he used his mouth on her. That as much as anything else might have been bothering Marty Cort, knowing that when Landergott went upstairs he got in bed with his China gal. Still, he had made his choice when asked to, and it wasn't his fault that he'd had to kill the older woman. As far as he was concerned, a bargain was a bargain.

Jesus, just thinking about that gal upstairs made his

dick stand up straight and stiff.

"It's only been two days," Landergott said, two very enjoyable days for him.

"Where can they be looking?"

"Maybe they're looking on the mountain. Maybe they ain't figured out that we came back here with her. I guess maybe they was a little shocked when they got back, huh?"

"A little, huh?" Cort asked, pouring himself a drink and depositing as much on the table as he did in the glass.

"Isn't it time for you to go up and spell Longtree on the roof?"

"Soon," Cort said. "One more drink."

"Yeah."

"Hey, Steve."

"What?"

"How about sharing with a buddy?"

"Sharing what?"

"You know. The girl!"

"Stop thinking about it, Marty. You'll make yourself crazy."

"Sure, make *myself* crazy." He downed his drink and stood up to go and relieve Longtree. He almost fell over, had to grab the table for support.

"Jesus, Marty, do you have to drink so much?"

"What else's there ta do?" Cort asked.

"Go upstairs and wake Cole and have him relieve Longtree."

"He complains that his wound hurts when he's on the roof."

"At least both his eyes will be open and he'll be able to see straight. Go wake him up and then sleep it off."

"Sure, Sheriff, an'thing you say, Steve boy."

Cort called Landergott "Sheriff" because as soon as they had returned the first thing he had done was kill the sheriff so they wouldn't have to worry about him getting brave and trying something. Now, Landergott wore the sheriff's badge.

Cort started for the steps, tripped on the first one, fell on his face, got up, and slowly went up the steps. Landergott watched him on the balcony to make sure he didn't go near Sooni's and his room. He knew that Sooni would rather be called Donna, but he liked calling her by her Chinese name. It excited him even more.

Cort went into the room he shared with the other men, and soon after Weston came out, grumbling and buckling his gunbelt. He limped out of sight to relieve Longtree on the roof. Cort was probably still inside, fast asleep already.

A few moments later Longtree came down, complaining of hunger and thirst.

"Have the bartender fix you something," Landergott said, standing up. "I'm going upstairs."

"You sure spend a lot of time upstairs these days, Steve."

Landergott smiled and said, "I wonder why?"

THIRTY-FOUR

Before Clint left the house he checked on Ling, who was awake.

"How are you feeling?"

"Weak."

"You should be. You lost a lot of blood."

"Chang told me that . . . Mother is dead?"

"Yes."

"And Stoney?"

"Yes."

"Sooni?"

"She was taken, but I'm going to get her back."

"My father?"

Clint made a face.

"We'll talk about him another time, Ling. When I come back."

"What if you do not come back?"

"Then you and your brother will have to do what

167

you think is best. Take care of each other."

Chang walked in and heard the last remark.

"We will take care of each other, Clint," he said. "You take care of Sooni."

"I will," he said, putting his hand on Chang's shoulder. "With a little luck I'll be back with her tonight."

"Then we wish you . . . a lot of luck!" Chang said.

Clint grinned, tousled the boy's hair, and then left the house without exchanging any words with Papa Teng. He wanted to get this over with and get away from that old Chinaman as fast as he could.

Outside he stopped at his rig and took out a pair of army binoculars. He also tucked the Colt New Line, which he had taken from Soong Teng's dead hand, and stuck it in his belt, inside of his shirt.

He rode toward town, but stopped inside a stand of trees before entering the basin. Once he did that he'd be out in the open.

From the cover of those trees he put the binoculars to his eyes and scanned the town. Even for Turner's Basin, it seemed even quieter and more deserted than usual. He saw the man on the roof of the saloon and sat there watching for a while. While he watched another man came up and the first man left. At no time did anyone enter or leave the saloon.

They're in there, he thought, bringing the binoculars down. They're holed up and waiting for me. That would be the smart thing to do, since they knew who they were dealing with. If they lived, ate, and slept in that one building, and kept a lookout, then there would be no chance of him picking them off one by one.

He had told the boys that, with a little luck he'd

return that night with Sooni, but he knew now that wasn't true. The only way he was going to get in there to get her was at night, and on foot. Even then, the area of the basin around the town was so flat that with a decent moon there was still a danger that he'd be seen.

He remembered Stoney telling him that he knew ways of getting in and out of town without being seen. He wished now that he had asked him some of those ways.

He put the binoculars away in his saddlebags and decided to ride right into town. At the very least he could talk to Landergott and find out just what he'd settle for in exchange for Sooni's life.

THIRTY-FIVE

When Landergott entered the room Sooni rose onto
her knees on the bed. She was naked, and he drank
in the sight of her. The full, brown-tipped breasts,
the slightly convex belly, because she still had a little
baby fat on her, and that slant-eyed face framed by
midnight-black hair. His dick was throbbing in his
pants.

"I've been waiting for you," she said.

"I know."

"Please," she said, fingering herself, "take off your
pants."

He decided not to make her beg him for too long
this time. Besides, he wanted her bad, and he was
the one who didn't want to wait.

He discarded his gunbelt, pulled off his boots, then
unbuckled his pants and let them fall to the floor. He
got rid of his shirt, and then peeled off his long under-

wear. He was a huge man in every respect, and his erection was a monstrous thing, almost alive as it throbbed and pulsed.

She crawled off the bed and came to him, fell to her knees before him. She took his cock in both hands, stroked it lovingly. She flicked out her tongue and licked the spongy head, then opened her mouth and took it inside. She sucked it while making a fist around the base of his huge member. She began to suck, at the same time pumping with her fist.

He set his legs wide apart and wrapped his fingers in her hair. The girl had an incredible mouth, and he could feel her breast rubbing against his thigh, first her left against his right, then her right against his left. He figured she liked the way the hair felt against her nipples.

Her nipples . . .

As good as he felt with her mouth on him, he wanted *his* mouth on *her*. He wanted to taste her, to touch her. He knew that the longer he waited for his orgasm, the better she would make it for him.

"Up," he said, pulling her up by the hair. "Get on the bed."

"Yes," she said, "on the bed."

He watched her taut backside as she ran to the bed and jumped on it, spread-eagled herself for him.

He moved forward to join her and she grabbed for him, pulling him to her. He began to suck and slobber over her breasts and nipples, and she held his head and murmured to him. He worked his way down over her belly until his tongue was laving her moist pubis. When he'd had his fill of her he raised himself over her and poked her wet portal with the head of his cock, sliding himself into her slowly until he filled her up.

The first time he took her it had been violently, with no regard for her at all, slamming into her while she cried out, writhing beneath him. Now he took her in long, easy strokes, luxuriating in the slick feel of her as her insides squeezed him, milked him, pulled him toward his orgasm. The only thing that hadn't changed was that he still had no regard for her pleasure at all.

He felt his legs beginning to tremble as his release approached . . .

. . . and then there was a knock on the door.

"What the hell is it?" he demanded.

"It's Longtree, Steve. Weston says Adams is coming."

"Just Adams?" Landergott asked. He was holding himself above Sooni with one hand on either side, looking down at her breasts. There was a heavy sheen of sweat glistening on her skin.

"Alone and bold as you please," Longtree called out. "He's just riding up to town."

"How long?"

"He's taking his time, so we figure it should be about five minutes."

"All right," Landergott called out, still staring at Sooni's breasts and nipples, as if they were hypnotizing him. "I'll be out."

She was watching him from the bed.

"Come on," he said, feeling his legs trembling, "finish me."

He began to slam into her then, faster and faster. She brought her legs up and wrapped them around him, holding on, moving her hips with him, finally finding and matching his tempo. When he came he roared in her ear, emptied himself into her, and then rolled off her.

As he dressed he realized that Adams was coming to negotiate for her release. What Adams didn't know was that he'd never let this little gal go.

Never.

Maybe not even for the gold.

THIRTY-SIX

Clint stopped Duke right in front of the saloon, dismounted, and entered, watched by the man on the roof. There was a bartender behind the bar, the same man Clint had talked to about Landergott. He didn't think the man was working with Landergott, or he wouldn't have talked about him in the first place.

As Clint started to approach the bar two men came out onto the balcony and down the steps. One was a very large, blond man with a scar.

Both men came down to the saloon level, and then the other man moved away from the scarred man, who approached the bar.

"You're Landergott," Clint said.

"That's right, Adams."

"A beer?"

Landergott laughed and said, "Sure."

"Two beers," Clint told the bartender.

When the man brought them Landergott picked

his up and drank half of it.

"You've got a lot of sand coming in here like this."

"Doesn't take much," Clint said. "I'm here to listen to your terms."

"I told one of those Chinese whelps my terms."

"Yes, and then kicked him in the face."

"He deserved it."

"Maybe you'll try it with me, some time."

"My pleasure, but let's not forget what we were talking about."

"Donna."

"Yes," Landergott said, "Sooni," and Clint frowned at the use of Donna's Chinese name.

"What do you want for her?"

"Well, I have to admit, she's increased in value since I first . . . took her."

Clint recognized the double meaning that the statement had.

"You want the gold."

"Oh, yes."

"I don't know where it is."

"What about the old Chinaman? Where is he, by the way? After all, it is his daughter we're talking about."

"Well, actually, that's where you made your mistake."

Landergott frowned and looked over at the other man, who was standing on the other side of the room.

"What mistake?"

"I guess you don't know much about the Chinese."

"I don't know anything about them."

"Well, you see, in Chinese families the males have considerable value, while the females have virtually none."

"What the hell are you talking about?"

"If you wanted the old man to talk to you, you should have taken one of his sons. He values them more highly than a mere daughter."

"You mean, he ain't dealing?"

"No. He refuses . . . but I am."

"With what?"

"The location of the gold."

"You know where it is?"

"I know what the old man is looking for. I can tell you his landmark, and you can take it from there."

"How do I know you know what you're talking about?"

"Because I wouldn't walk in here and risk my neck with bad information."

Landergott was frowning and looking at the other men.

"Where are the rest of your friends?" Clint asked.

"They're around, and I'll have to talk to them about this."

"Well, sure you will." Clint finished his beer and put the empty mug down on the bar. He couldn't make a move because there were two men missing. For all he knew, one of them could be with Donna / Sooni. If something went wrong, he might have instructions to kill her. "I'll come back later for your answer."

"Tomorrow," Landergott said. "Come back in the morning. I'll tell you what we're going to do, then."

"All right, in the morning."

Clint turned and walked away from the bar toward the batwing doors. When he reached them he turned back to Landergott, who was still standing at the bar.

"By the way . . ."

"Yeah?"

"Where is she?"

"You'd like to know, wouldn't you?"

"I'd like to know that she's all right."

"Believe me," Landergott said with a smirk, "she's just fine."

"I'll take your word for that now," Clint said, "but before I hand over any information I'll want to see her."

"You'll see her," Landergott said, "tomorrow."

Clint stared at Landergott, then nodded and walked out, outwardly much calmer than he felt.

He had no intentions of waiting until the morning.

After Clint Adams left, Longtree came over to the bar and told the bartender to give him a beer.

"What do you think?" he asked.

"He knows. He's been with that old man for a long time. He knows."

"And he'll tell us."

"Oh yes, he will," Landergott said. "In the morning. He'll see the girl, give us the information . . . and then he'll die."

THIRTY-SEVEN

Clint did not get as far as his horse.

He stopped on the boardwalk just outside the saloon and said aloud, "Oh, hell. Why not?"

He decided right then and there not to push his luck. He'd gotten into town without any problem. It might not be that easy to come back at night. He was here now, he might as well get it over with.

He turned around and walked back in.

Landergott was still standing at the bar and the other man had moved to the stairs, which he was about to ascend.

"You forget something?" Landergott asked.

"Yeah. I forgot who I was."

"Who are you?"

"The Gunsmith."

"Is that supposed to frighten me?"

Clint shrugged. He didn't normally use his reputation this way, but he figured he might as well use everything that was at his disposal.

"Maybe it would make you smarter if you thought about it some more."

Landergott shook his head.

"I got too much riding here to back off because of a rep, Adams."

"Okay, so don't back off, but I want to see the girl—now!"

"I told you tomorrow."

"And I just told you now."

They stared at each other, and Clint could see the other man from the corner of his eye. He was watching his leader, Landergott, waiting for his move.

Suddenly, Landergott smiled.

"All right," he agreed. "I'll let you see the girl." He raised his chin and shouted, "Sooni!"

It only took one shout and Sooni came out onto the balcony—naked.

"Donna, are you all right?" Clint asked.

"Hi, Clint," she said, putting her hands on the balcony railing and leaning on them. Her breasts were plainly in view, and Clint saw the other man staring at them.

"Are you all right?" he asked again.

"I'm fine."

"I've come to get you away."

"Away from what?"

Clint frowned.

"Away from Landergott."

"What makes you think I want to get away?"

"I don't understand . . ." he said, even though he thought that perhaps he did.

"How do you think I found out about the gold in the first place?" Landergott asked.

"From her?"

"Sure."

"Donna?"

"Yes, I told him. I knew he wanted me, so I made the gold a condition."

"I can't believe this," he said. "You betrayed your father, your family?"

"I didn't betray them," she said. "I just want to get away from them."

"This man killed your mother."

"It . . . was an accident."

"No, it wasn't."

"That's enough," Landergott said. "It's out in the open now, so there's no need for negotiation. I want to know what you know about the location of the gold."

"Forget it."

"What?"

"You said it yourself. There's no need for negotiation. You keep the girl, and I'll keep the gold."

"Landergott—" the other man said.

"Easy, Longtree," Landergott said. To Clint he said, "You ain't walking out of here, Adams, if I don't get that information."

"You got that wrong, Landergott," Clint said, spreading his feet for leverage. "It's you who isn't walking out."

"Well," Landergott said, "there's always the Chinaman."

Clint saw Landergott's hand move, and knew that the man called Longtree would only be a second or two behind.

That was plenty of time for him.

He drew his gun in a fraction of a second and fired at Landergott first. The bullet struck the big man in the chest before he could even reach his gun. Clint turned quickly and fired at Longtree. The bullet punched a hole just above the man's right eye and he fell onto the steps with his gun still holstered.

"Clint! Look out!" he heard Donna call.

He looked up and saw a man pointing a gun at him. He threw himself to the floor as the man fired, rolled, came up on his knee, and fired. His bullet hit the man just below the base of the throat, causing him to drop his gun and then tumble over the railing.

Clint stood up, his gun ready, looking around. The bartender had dropped behind the bar when the shooting started, and didn't seem to pose any danger.

He looked up at Donna and it did not escape his attention that she had very probably saved his life.

"Any more?"

"One," she said. "He must be in his room."

Clint ran up the steps and joined her on the balcony.

"Which room?" he asked.

She pointed to a door and said, "That one."

"Get dressed."

She went back in her room to do so, and Clint moved to the other door. He put his ear to it and thought he heard something. When he opened the door he discovered that he had heard correctly.

There was a man lying on a bed, fully dressed, snoring loudly. Clint approached the bed and removed the man's gun, which was still strapped to his hip. He looked around and saw no other weapons in the room, so he left the man asleep and vacated the room.

Donna was waiting on the balcony, fully dressed.

"You want to explain this to me?" he asked.

"What is there to explain? I thought Landergott was my way out. Later, I thought it was you, but when you refused I went back to considering Landergott."

"And the gold?"

"Yes. Papa doesn't need the gold. He has his sons."

"And what now, with Landergott dead?"

She shrugged.

"He was a pig anyway. I had to pretend to enjoy being with him when he took me, because he wasn't sure how I would react to what happened at the house."

"And how did you react?"

"I'm sorry my mother is dead, Clint. I did love her. The first chance I had once we had the gold I probably would have killed Landergott."

"You think you could do that? Kill a man?"

"I guess I will never know."

"I hope you won't," he said sincerely. "Are you ready to go home?"

She sighed and said, "Yes."

As they walked down the stairs she said, "What about you, and me, and the gold?"

"Forget it. If you want to get away, Donna—or Sooni—"

"Donna," she said.

"—you'll just have to walk away yourself."

"I might," she said. "I really might."

They rounded up a horse for Donna and then rode back to the house. It was an hour from dark when they reached it, and he realized that he had been true to his word to the boys, after all.

When they entered the house Chang saw Donna and rushed into her arms. She hugged the boy tightly, and Clint felt that she actually loved her brothers. She was probably a very confused young woman.

Chang took Donna in to see Ling, and then came out to see Clint.

"Chang, where is your father?"

Chang looked at the floor, then back at Clint.

"He went looking for the gold."

"Damn him!"

Chang jumped in reaction to Clint's vehemence.

"I'm sorry, Chang. I realize he's your father—"

Donna came out at that point and put her arm around the boy's shoulders.

"What's wrong?"

"I warned your father what would happen if he left these boys alone to look for that gold."

"He went, anyway," she said. It was a statement of fact, not a question.

"Yes."

"I am not surprised, Clint. You should not be, either."

"No, I guess not."

She looked at her brother and said, "You must be hungry."

"Yes."

"They haven't been eating very well since—since you left."

"I will see what I can prepare."

She managed to find the fixings for some soup. It was dark and she, Chang, and Clint were sitting down to dinner—Ling was eating in bed—when the door opened and Papa Teng walked in.

Right away Clint knew something had happened because the old man's eyes were shining. He actually looked *excited*.

"Papa—" Donna said.

He didn't even look at her. Instead, he fixed Clint with a somewhat triumphant glare.

"I found it!"

THIRTY-EIGHT

The next morning Clint and Papa Teng left early. Papa could hardly contain himself, and it was not a Papa Teng that Clint could adjust himself to.

They left Donna to care for the two boys, and Clint took Duke and one of the team horses. He intended to use the team horse as a pack horse to bring back at least some of the gold.

"They are gold coins," Papa Teng said as they worked their way up the mountain. "They gleam, even in the darkness of the cave."

"Was your friend Khan's landmark correct?"

"Yes. I found three caves, one directly above the other. I found the gold in the center cave."

"So then I guess you've got what you want, Papa Teng."

Papa Teng didn't reply.

"There it is," he said sometime later.

"We won't get the horses up there," Clint said. "What is the gold in?"

"Saddlebags."

"Good. That will make it easy to transport."

Papa Teng wasn't listening, however. He was already clambering up the side of the slope. Having made the climb before he seemed to know the way, so Clint followed in his wake.

By the time Clint reached the level of the second cave, he was entering it himself when he heard a shriek from inside. He drew his gun and rushed inside.

"No, no, no!" Papa Teng was shouting when Clint reached him. "It was here, I know it was here. I saw it yesterday." He turned to Clint and said desperately, "The gold was here!"

Clint looked around the cave and saw no saddlebags, and no gold. He did, however, see signs that someone had been in the cave recently. There were a couple of leather straps that looked as if they had come off a saddlebag, and a couple of buckskin fringes that seemed to have been torn off by sharp rocks on the side of the cave.

Clint recalled that some of the Indians he had seen after he killed the wolf had been wearing buckskin jackets.

"It was here, I know it was," Papa Teng was saying, moving in circles, searching the floor.

"Well, it's not here now, Papa Teng," Clint said, holstering his gun. "Looks like your Indian friends found it at about the same time you did."

Papa Teng turned and stared at Clint in disbelief.

"The Indians?"

"Who else could it be?"

"You! You took my gold!"

"Don't be ridiculous, Papa. I didn't leave the house last night. Face it. The Indians either found it themselves, or saw you come in here. They took the gold."

"But that is not fair! What would the Indians want with gold?"

"Indians are not stupid, Papa. They know they can use gold to get the things they want."

"Indians!" Papa Teng grabbed Clint's arm and said, "We must find them."

"You find them," Clint said. "I'm finished, Papa Teng. I'm leaving in the morning. If I was you I'd start thinking about the family I have left. Your sons *and* your daughter."

"But how will we live?"

"The way you did before you caught gold fever," Clint said. "You'll work, and so will your children. Lots of people survive that way, Papa."

Moving as if he were still stunned, Papa Teng walked toward the front of the cave. Clint was about to follow when he decided to walk around the cave one time. As he did, he found some loose gold coins lying on the floor of the cave which Papa Teng, in his panic, had missed. Apparently, one of the saddlebags must have had a hole in it. He followed the trail of coins toward the front of the cave, where it stopped. The hole must have been discovered.

He looked down into his hands and saw that he had picked up a dozen gold coins. He put them in his pockets, having already decided what he would do with them. He wouldn't keep them, and he wouldn't give them to Papa Teng. He would give four each to Sooni, Ling, and Chang. After that it would be up to them what they would do with them. He hoped that they would all make the right decision and use the coins for the good of the entire family.

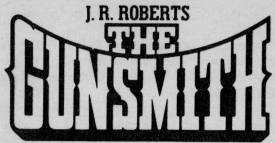

J. R. ROBERTS
THE GUNSMITH
SERIES

Please send the titles I've checked above. Mail orders to:

BERKLEY PUBLISHING GROUP
390 Murray Hill Pkwy., Dept. B
East Rutherford, NJ 07073

NAME_____

ADDRESS_____

CITY_____

STATE_____ ZIP_____

Please allow 6 weeks for delivery.
Prices are subject to change without notice.

POSTAGE & HANDLING:
$1.00 for one book, $.25 for each
additional. Do not exceed $3.50.

BOOK TOTAL	$_____
SHIPPING & HANDLING	$_____
APPLICABLE SALES TAX (CA, NJ, NY, PA)	$_____
TOTAL AMOUNT DUE	$_____

PAYABLE IN US FUNDS.
(No cash orders accepted.)